NORTH EAST of SCOTLAND LIBRARY SERVICE
MELDRUM MEG WAY, OLDMELDRUM

KNIGHT, ALANNA

This outward angel

SFR

MYS

483547

N E S L S
483547

This Outward Angel

This Outward
Angel

Alanna Knight

MYS
483547

This title first published in Great Britain 1993 by
SEVERN HOUSE PUBLISHERS LTD of
9–15 High Street, Sutton, Surrey SM1 1DF
First published in the U.S.A. 1993 by
SEVERN HOUSE PUBLISHERS INC of
475 Fifth Avenue, New York, NY 10017.

British Library Cataloguing in Publication Data
Knight, Alanna
  This Outward Angel
  I. Title
  823.914 [F]

  ISBN 0-7278-4483-0

All situations in this publication are fictitious and
any resemblance to living persons is purely coincidental.

Typeset by Hewer Text Composition Services, Edinburgh.
Printed and bound in Great Britain by
Dotesios Ltd, Trowbridge, Wiltshire.

"O, what may man within him hide,
Though angel on the outward side!"
William Shakespeare,
Measure for Measure,
(Act III, ii, 293.)

Chapter 1

The North Sea was a hyacinth-blue line, deftly drawn by a celestial artist, clever but inhuman. With frightening perfection it stretched across a razor-edge of horizon, infinite, eternal. The sun blazed inland and the celestial artist, now color blind, faded green of grass, blue of sky, to blend with a monotone of blurred spires, granite-gray and spectral.

Aberdeen in a heatwave, dazedly living up (for once) to a brochured reputation as "The Silver City with the Golden Sands."

Tomorrow, warned the weathermen, there will be rain. But on the day I left the bus and climbed the steep hill overlooking the River Dee, the roads danced, shimmering with mirage-like pools of fast-melting tar. The smell of tar vied with roses and new-cut grass, as lawn-mowers noisily grazed, fretting away the drowsy hours of a hot Saturday afternoon, their uncouth sounds angrily dispersing those more natural to summer.

Bored insects, inert with heat, sleepily performed their botanical duty by assaulting neat clumps of flowers and, exhausted by a particularly prolific summer of nesting, no birds sang, or flew, or were even visible.

The council estate lay straight ahead, bleached white under the sun, exotic and frivolous as a Greek island from a travel poster. Until one observed the stern Presbyterian zeal with which streets, crescents, avenues and drives issued forth named for Reformation martyrs and

1

long-dead Calvinists. The sentiment seemed overdone but the view across Aberdeen's distant spires was superb, especially from my bedroom window in the crowded little semi-detached I shared with Dad, my stepmother Pearl, their twin girls, small boy and two dogs.

I was more than usually aware of the dark unease of doubts and fears today. Perhaps the final straw was having bought a wildly expensive purple dress at the new boutique. Besides making my carrot-red hair wince, it was an ill-advised sales bargain. With my present job about to fold, I should not have been on a lavish spending spree . . .

Oh, worry tomorrow, I told myself. Enjoy the heatwave while it lasts. Pretend the back garden is your Greek island (where you should have been with Fiona right now.)

We had talked of nothing else but the cruise all winter, an exceptionally grim, snowy, bleak Aberdeen winter. In the office, at the discos (where the men were never the men we wanted), or walking along the Promenade at weekends with our heads well down into coat collars and a mass of leaflets clutched in our icy fingers.

On one such day we rescued a small black dog from a watery grave. She had enlivened the months since by being the subject of some vituperation between Stepmother Pearl and myself. For to Pearl with a Balmoral-born corgi (whom she loved to hint was of the dog-blood Royal), a mongrel was the final insult.

The Isles of Greece. How wonderfully romantic . . . Then one day Fiona fell in love and a late summer wedding was imminent. Heaven knows I didn't begrudge her happiness, but in twenty-three years curiously doomed to transient relationships, I would miss our year-old pleasant companionship. Even if it were my own fault for accepting protestations like: "I'm nearly twenty-seven . . . marriage is not for me . . . all the nicest men are married." And her favorite: "Unless he's quite exceptional, I would be bored to death with most men. My ideal is wildly artistic, superbly handsome – you know, Lucinda, the kind of man one never meets in real life . . ."

I knew indeed. So except to hint at a broken love affair, I was silent about Drew. Drew, who fitted her requirements admirably. Quite exceptional, he was the kind of man no other human being should *ever* have to meet in real life.

He was the only secret between us. If Fiona had not spoken and at times behaved exactly like the daughter of a Jane Austen rector, then I could and would have told her. But her prim manner discouraged any discussion of sex, turning it into an embarrassing description of the messy details of an intimate operation (which in fact, was the only way to describe my brief marriage to Drew). Or maybe the reason for silence lay deeper. That life and sanity depended on forgetting, on burying the past so completely that I could pretend that Drew never existed.

Fervently now, I could thank God that he existed no longer. Except as a segment of tortured memory to erupt in dreams. I would open a door, find him there, alive and waiting . . . beckoning, gently smiling . . . and I'd wake up sweating with terror.

Odd that I didn't relish Dad's move last year from Newcastle to Aberdeen, simply because once, long ago Drew had mentioned relatives in Aberdeen. Not that kinship was a thing he set store by and he held them, as he held all humanity, in utmost contempt, but high on pot or alcohol, he sometimes bragged of their descent from King Macbeth. I dismissed it all as yet another colorful fantasy, for Drew would never willingly tell tame truth if an elaborate frightening lie would serve.

Danger . . . Danger . . .

A red light flashed by the roadside. What was it, an accident? Only a warning to traffic, I discovered. The corporation arrived secretly, mysteriously ripped up estate roads and replaced them in exactly the same positions, all with monotonous frequency. As if reports of buried treasure had come their way and could not afford to be ignored.

Danger indeed. Danger was a story one read in the warm security of an armchair by the fire on a winter's night. Danger didn't belong to high summer and an uneventful life in an Aberdeen suburb among rows of identical houses with neat pretty gardens. One flirted with danger vicariously in thrillers, or watched – clammy-handed but unassailable, from a seat in the balcony: "The Vampire Strikes Back," "Secrets from Frankenstein's Grave." Once only had it touched me personally, the gust of pure horror fluttering small uneasy wings across a nightmare of days and nights with Drew.

He was the nearest approximation to a real, live, flesh-and-blood ghoul, a super sadist. Even three years apart had not blunted the worst episodes, the tearing-off of wings from his human butterfly, the poisoning of every decency in which I believed.

But this magic summer had freed me. For ever now I was safe, safe from my tormentor, safe from the past. The butterfly although severely wounded, might yet live out her day. A month ago I had been persuaded to go with the family to a rented cottage on Skye, where wild Wagnerian sunsets competed with torrential rain in the wettest summer for years. I was duly installed as dish-washer, nurse and baby-sitter, my "consolation" (said Pearl) for "missing Greece."

One afternoon Dad drove back from the village and silently handed me a two-day old national newspaper: "Train Disaster in South of England." Among the list of those killed was Drew Mervyn. That was his stage name. Our marriage under the family name was kept secret. There was mercifully nothing to connect him with me.

Dad watched my face as I read it. "I'm glad the bastard's dead, after what he did to you," he said, with vehemence

4

surprising in so mild a man. Surprising too, considering he only knew part of it, the milder, more decently describable atrocities. He gripped my shoulder, said anxiously, "You're all right now, lass? Over it all, aren't you?"

"Of course. Long ago," I said, smiling and patted his hand. But behind that smile I remembered Tony. My only regret that Drew's dear inseparable partner-in-evil, Tony, hadn't accompanied him on that last fatal journey. In that way, so easily, could the world had been rid of two monsters.

Danger . . . Danger . . . winked the road sign, growing depressingly closer, larger. Behind it the tinkle of laughter. A wedding party in the street taking pictures of a radiant bride in her white veil, the elaborate brocades and velvets incongruous against the simplicity of a sunny garden. Everyone was happy, transported by the intoxication of love. I walked past, waved and wished them well, thanking God that love was an addiction to which I was now immune.

Just to please Fiona, to make Dad happy and console Pearl (that I wouldn't be around the house for ever), I made noises of being interested in "meeting someone." But my heart wasn't in it, and love could be measured sadly by the hour, as every man I met struck some unfortunate chord of remembrance. After all, hadn't Drew started off with a pretense of normal courtship and love? The same overtures, the same delectable sounds?

Behind the flowers, the telephone calls and tender attentions, my quivering antennae were quick to detect another monster in the making. Quick to see my innocent, unfortunate suitor through eyes that had beheld the utmost in human degradation. The romantic scales would speedily drop from my eyes. "Just in time," I'd tell Fiona.

"What do you mean? He's only human, poor lad." And she would give me a terrible lecture on her favorite cliché.

5

"Nobody's perfect, you know." Or "You can't blame all men just because one made you unhappy."

Unhappy. Oh, how mild the word. Unhappy was something one associated with the normal everyday misfortunes in life. Toothache, a cold in the head, a domestic quarrel, the death of a beloved pet. But unhappy was a senseless, meaningless word to describe the undescribable horror of an inhuman marriage.

"There are some good, nice men in the world, Lucinda. Life can't be over for you at twenty-three. You're letting bitterness warp your soul," Fiona lectured sternly, forgetting that the soul too can die. And unable to frame the words to defeat her evangelistic efforts that would set my feet firmly back on the road to truth and beauty, I would tell her:

"I don't want a leading role in the strong emotions of life. Not even a teeny walk-on part. Not to worry, Fiona, I'm not complaining. I'm happy as a bystander –"

"But it's not natural –"

(Ah yes, but it is. A lot more natural than it was.) So I assured her I was content with the family and a comfortable home. Small, perhaps, a bit overcrowded, but mine as long as I needed it. Dad had so sworn when, broken and ill, three years ago, I had come home wanting only a quiet place to die.

"Dick says you ought . . . Dick says you must . . ."

How often these days did I yawn, as the ungrateful beneficiary of Dick's foraging into psychology. Dick was a newly graduated doctor and, life being nothing if not ironical, the very antithesis of all Fiona's stern pronouncements on the "exceptional qualities" she required in a man. Dick was nice, kind, well-behaved and ordinary to a striking degree. The men we met were all nice, kind, well-behaved and ordinary.

With only one exception.

A strange, striking face, briefly glimpsed at a students'

6

springtime dance. I was fascinated, attracted by the honest ugliness of a face all angles, high cheekbones and wide slanting dark eyes.

Fiona stared at me. "Fascinating – him? Surely not. You must be joking. How could anyone possibly consider him attractive. He's so – so barbaric-looking. Like a gypsy. Lucinda, you don't mean it – he's quite *ugly* . . ."

Ugly, perhaps, I thought. But the furthest I could run from Drew's satanic beauty or Tony's dainty elegance.

"Anyway, he looks foreign to me," said Fiona suspiciously.

I thought so too, but when I heard him speak, there was no accent. "He looks like an Aztec warrior from an old painting," I said.

Fiona shuddered. "Trust you to pick someone like that. He certainly looks savage enough."

"Hamish was talking to him at the bar," I said significantly. Hamish was then her latest love, and Dick's immediate predecessor.

"All right, if you insist. I can take the hint. I'll get you an introduction. But don't blame me for what happens, remember I warned you." She wagged an admonishing finger at me. "He doesn't look as if he knows the meaning of 'no' for an answer. He probably eats gentle, sweet girls like you every day."

"Idiot," I shouted after her. She came back clinging to Hamish's arm, alone. "Too late, alas, alack," she whispered. "See for yourself, Lucinda dear."

And there at a corner table was my Barbaric Stranger, smooching with a very pretty girl with long, lint-colored hair.

"I see what you mean by eating them up."

Later when the music took a romantic turn, they danced past, clinging together. The girl whispered, and the stern lines of his face melted.

7

"Heigh ho, Fiona," I sighed. "You must admit he has a lovely smile."

"Heigh ho, nothing. It's too full of teeth for my liking. Oh, here's Hamish," she said happily indicating that the contrast reassured her. Hamish had eyes for no girl but her and was already regretting the generous impulse of inviting her to bring along a friend. Now pathetically eager to get rid of my presence for the journey home, he had spent an entire evening emerging from the bar, leading like reluctant shire horses at a show, a succession of acquaintances for my approval. The latest capture was a thin, tall nervous-looking young man with hair as carrot-red as my own.

"Make do with this one," said Fiona. "He's been watching you for hours. Lucky old you, he's fantastically rich," she lied encouragingly.

Before we had even reached the floor together, Hamish had heard opportunity's knock and was disappearing fast with Fiona through the exit. My partner's height was a disadvantage strategically producing an Adam's apple which bobbed nervously up and down directly in my line of vision. I discovered his passions in life were stamps, Cairngorm stones and chess. As none of these activities turned me on, all sensible conversation died.

Driven home in a handsome sports car, I was kissed goodnight in the sharp, rather bad-tempered way of one whose heart wasn't in it, but considered such behavior as a duty and moreover, good for the image of a rich young man who was trendy and with-it. We parted with a sense of relief, which was, I'm sure, mutual.

This was the memorable night Fiona fell out with Hamish and fell in with Dick. So I never did get my introduction to the Barbaric Stranger.

However, after that first glimpse, he showed an increasing tendency to turn up in the most unexpected places (probably he had always been there but I hadn't noticed him before). I saw him on buses, browsing in bookshops, even once walking along the beach with a long-haired blonde who wasn't the one at the dance. Then he became almost accessible, by playing an electric guitar in a three-piece band at the twenty-first birthday party of one of our student friends. Surprisingly too, he sang, his voice pleasant, deep, but unremarkable. Tall, slim and dark, the distant impression was of an exotic Tom Jones or Englebert, a fascinating combination of sensuality and aestheticism, for he had a curious immobility, as if he fed on some inner fire.

When I asked my hostess who he was, she shrugged: "Don't know, sorry. Daddy booked them."

It was a hot night, steamy as the tropics, the suite in the Beach Ballroom thick with smoke. The singer shed his suede jacket and the white shirt open to the waist, somehow emphasized his barbarity, his remoteness. Then at the song's end, he made a light gesture with his hand and I noticed the thunderbird around his neck.

A thunderbird of gold, with turquoises for wings and eyes. It wasn't until much later that I realized in semi-darkness and in that one small gesture, I couldn't possibly have recognised it as *The* Thunderbird.

Chilled to the very roots of my being, I stopped dancing and my partner trod heavily on my toes. Taking his cheek and heavy breathing away from my ear he said, "What's wrong? What *are* you shivering about?"

Shakily I laughed and applauded the singer. "Geese on my grave, I expect." But all the way home I knew there was something more than that. The thunderbird belonged to a recurring dream, of a time and place beyond this earth. A red desert with monstrous rocks and horsemen. Death . . . Danger . . .

Danger, danger, winked the road sign. "Oh, you silly thing. Danger is just a traffic warning, the feeling in your bones is nonsense. It *has* to be nonsense.

"Danger died with Drew. The past is finished.

"Think of the present, girl, you have problems enough. Before this summer is over, you have to find another job."

Small wonder I was depressed, imagining things. Change of any kind frightened me now. Life with Dad and Pearl and the children provided the illusion of security, a safe shell around me, even my own small dog to be taken for walks at night. Slowly from the ruin Drew had left my life, I was building a wall of safety, normality – by not falling in love, not risking anything that whispered of the wind of change, or danger.

But this summer, Fiona was going. The pleasant but dull importer's office we shared was closing down. I had to make other friends, build another background. And I was scared. Scared to death.

Turning my back on the road sign with its gloomy prophecy, I had arrived in John Knox Avenue where a huge black limousine took up half the street. Home. I sighed. Safe and secure. Idiotic to believe that even Destiny would have the energy (on an afternoon like this) to stalk one small insignificant girl in an Aberdeen suburb.

Safe and secure. There was the neat little house with the frilly curtains Pearl had made, the pretty garden . . .

Then I noticed the black limousine. It wasn't waiting at the house next door as I had imagined. It was outside our gate.

I looked back down the hill. Far beyond the winking red light of danger, somewhere on the hyacinth blue horizon, a dark sinister bank of mist billowed inwards and like the voice of doom the foghorn's gloomy wail cut across the searing heat of the afternoon.

Danger . . . Danger . . .

Chapter 2

The visitor had been unexpected. There were Dad's precious gardening tools hastily abandoned and at the mercy of three-year old Timmy, luckily more absorbed by clinging to the gate and mournfully reviewing the inadequacies of his own pedal car as compared with the black shiny car at the curb.

Timmy also showed unmistakeable signs of having been taken by surprise, in his most tattered "play" shorts, with a very grubby face. Stepmother Pearl usually scrubbed him until his naturally technicolored face shone like a well-polished rosy apple and had him walking stiff at the knees, the fear of death (and Pearl's heavy hand) put into him that he'd fall and spoil the absurd clothes (including knee-length white socks and shoes), she kept for his "best."

"Hello, Timmy." Absentmindedly he responded to my hug and kiss today, totally unable to drag his eyes away, torn between envy and reproach, for that lovely car.

"Man gone inside," he said importantly.

As I opened the front door, ten pounds of dense black wool hurtled downstairs and into my arms. That dog, or TeeDee the Unbeautiful, rescued from a watery death at Nigg, frantically but silently licked my face, her stump of a tail mad with joy.

"Going to play with Timmy?" She understood every word I said to her, and a lot I didn't say but only felt. She put her head on the side, gazed into the garden, raised a paw, heard Pearl's voice and rushed back upstairs to her basket in my bedroom. TeeDee might have dubious ancestry but her manners were straight from the top drawer. She knew every flicker of Pearl's uncertain temper and, with split-second precision, when it behove her to make herself scarce.

I closed the front door, deciding that salesmen these days have a super time. This one was probably on an encyclopedia kick, or selling double glazing. But as soon as I reached the living-room door, I knew there was something more than that. There was an attractive man around somewhere. There had to be. The air was thick with an overdose of Pearl's favorite perfume and an overdose of what Fiona called her "scenty voice" reverberated through the wall. High-pitched, it carried clear through the house, the "turribly po-late" voice she kept for those she considered her betters.

I really liked Pearl, she was only ten years my senior. ("How lucky you are, you must be such friends," said those fortunate enough not to share the same roof with us.) We should have been friends, she was as mod and trendy as I could have wished, but somehow friendship was quite beyond us. We quarrelled, noisily and often. Dad would come home, sigh, put an arm around us both and say:

"Blest if I know what to do, or what's wrong with either of you. Why can't you get along together, you're both good lasses?"

Perhaps our basic incompatibility was based on jealousy. Fiona had decided long ago that this was the cause, because I was Dad's first child and according to everyone, very like Mum who had died so tragically before I could ever know her. Dad forgave me for my unintentional part in the sad little drama (which was saying a lot because he had adored her). An attractive man still at fifty, he waited a long time to marry Pearl, who adored him. So did the twins, Jane and Emma, beautiful blue-eyed blonde angels, picture-book

12

children. Even at twelve, they were the vainest children one could wish to meet.

Since the advent of TeeDee, Pearl and I were in perpetual ferment and Fiona's Monday morning remark in the office was usually "How's Wicked Stepmother this morning? Still treading on Snow White's toes?"

"If only I were Snow White," I'd say, ruefully tackling long thick carrot-red hair with a sturdy comb and dabbing green shadow above eyes which in kinder light were hazel, on sad days, merely mud-colored.

"All this and freckles too. There's only one thing wrong with your fairy story, Fiona dear. It's the Wicked Step-mother and the Ugly Sisters who are the beauties, Snow White is the Ugly Duckling strode on to the wrong set."

"Come off it," said Fiona. "You've got gorgeous eyes and you're not all that bad-looking. You're trim and neat –"

"But hardly curvaceous," I said, straightening a skinny-rib sweater with little to show under it and eyeing Fiona's ample bosom with envy.

"Better too little than too much. Like me," she groaned.

Now Pearl dashed out of the living-room, looking seventeen and delectable. "What's all this?" I asked. "Fee fi fo fum, I smell the blood of an attractive man."

She gave me a dagger-like look and dragging at my arm said loudly (for the unseen visitor's benefit), "Oh, here you are at last, Lucinda darling. Had a good day, dear? Did you get my messages? Ha ha." And thrusting me unceremoniously into the kitchen, she closed the door and said in her normal voice, "C'mon, till I tell you."

"What gives?" I asked somewhat crustily, rubbing bruised fingers and thrusting the psychedelic paper bag bearing purple dress out of sight.

But Stepmother wasn't interested. There were none of the usual acid comments about wasting my money when I should have been saving it until I got another job and that my father couldn't be expected to keep me.

"For heaven's sake, Pearl, *who* have you got in there?"

She stared at the door, wide-eyed and whispered. "Shut up and listen. You'll never guess. It's your uncle. Elliott MacAeden," she added triumphantly.

I gripped the kitchen table for support. Now I knew why the air had turned suddenly to ice and in the silence that followed, the foghorn bleated its solemn warning twice through the still sunny room.

"Never heard of him," I said lightly, wondering how in heaven's name I could escape this encounter.

"You must have," she said disbelievingly. "Try to remember, you must. He's your – your late husband's cousin – or something. And what's more, this is your big chance, Lucinda. Because from what I can see, he's rolling in money. Just think, play your cards well, and you need never work again."

"Hold on, hold on. You're way ahead of me. Is that his car outside?"

"Yes. He lives in Lairigbrach."

"The Lairigbrach. On the Deeside Road?"

"Of course, stupid. And he's – very – interested – " she stopped to stab a finger at me – "in *you*."

"Whatever for?"

"Oh, use your head. Because Drew was a MacAeden."

"So what? What's so special about being a MacAeden. There are probably millions of them, like MacIntoshes and MacDonalds."

She shook her head. "No. That's exactly it. There's only you, I gather." She paused significantly. "Don't you realize what this means? You may be an heiress or something."

"An heiress." I tried to let the implication sink in but it floated away obstinately, refusing to make sense.

"An heiress," repeated Pearl with satisfaction. "There now."

14

"You mean the man in there talking to Dad is a rich uncle, just like those corny old movies," I said and when she nodded vigorously, "You must have blown your tiny transistor, Pearl love. He's putting you on. Probably a white slaver, after the twins."

It was mean and she paled visibly. Just in time Dad poked his head around the door. "Come on, Lucy. What's keeping you two gossiping in here? Thought you were making tea, Pearl?"

"So I was. Except that *your* daughter keeps trying to be funny. I'm just about dead laughing. I suppose she gets the sense of humor from you," she added nastily, snapping on the kettle.

"Come and meet him," said Dad. And noticing my hesitation he squeezed my arm. "Don't worry, love, it'll be all right. Besides he seems a nice sort of old chap." So between Pearl and Dad, like a condemned prisoner I was marched towards the living room.

I don't know what I expected when Dad opened the door. Certainly not the rather shrivelled little old man with gray hair (what was left of it), a gray mustache and the kind of face I'd unhesitantly call "ferrety." He certainly wasn't a stirring sight and I began to wonder if I had been too far out with the white-slaving idea. And then he turned to me and smiled and I saw his eyes.

I took a step backwards. Those eyes were to use the old cliché, Drew's eyes exactly. Whoever this man was, he was most certainly Drew's relation.

He took my hand, bowed over it and said, "Mrs MacAeden."

And I shuddered to the very soles of my feet, as if the past had stretched out and laid a skeleton hand on my shoulder. It was three years since anyone had called me Mrs MacAeden, neither friends nor family, who knew how anxious I was to forget. He must have mistaken my convulsive start for grief because he took my other hand gently, like someone consoling a small child.

"My dear, I'm so sorry. We all are. But why didn't you get in touch with us before? I realize Rosanna disapproved of her nephew's marriage – to *anyone*. A terribly possessive woman, you know, considered Drew *her* property, since she had adopted him as a child. Could hardly abide to let him out of her sight; the only time we ever had him for holidays was when she went off gallivanting back to Australia. However, I mustn't bore you with stories about Rosanna. Didn't Drew tell you about the rest of the family, up here in Scotland?"

"No. You realize we were separated – for three years now," I added gently. Surely he must have known? How otherwise did he explain my non-appearance at Drew's funeral?

"Oh, that," he dismissed it with a wave of his hand. "I know what it's like in the theater. People come and go. You would have gone back together some day, I'm sure of it. Perhaps when you were both older and wiser and the fires had died down a little." He cleared his throat.

"As a matter of fact, I wasn't aware that Drew *had* a wife, until Rosanna told me, er, recently. She had never met you and was most unhelpful. Since then I have had the utmost difficulty in tracking you down."

He paused. "My dear, there was nothing to be ashamed of, nothing. I'm a very broad-minded man and this is a situation tragically frequent these days. We MacAedens have hardly the kind of family history where such, er, matters are unknown. And Drew was always a little wild," he added fondly, unable to keep the pride from his voice, smiling at me as if for confirmation.

There was nothing I could say. Nothing that would not wound this poor deluded man to the soul. I thought he was still talking about the separation until he added significantly:

16

"There *is* a child, I believe."

I began to tremble. Remembering in every hideous detail. I caught Pearl's disapproving eye and heard her sharp intake of breath. "Shotgun weddings" were for the notorious and the very poor. Respectable middle-class families had only premature births, complete to the last fingernail and eyelash, after only five months' gestation. Pearl got the significance of Elliott MacAeden's remarks and was shocked. Where she was concerned you traded in virginity like pink stamps, for marriage and your children were conceived in honeymoon hotels or in marriage beds, electric blanketed and all tied up with vows and blessed by state or church. Girls like Pearl were never seduced by a couple of drinks too many or the illusion that an hour's lust might turn out to be a lifetime's love.

"I believe Drew left a son," said Elliott MacAeden.

"Oh," said Pearl, but Dad shook his head, warningly.

"There *was* a child," I began and stopped. The words would not come.

Again hesitation was mistaken for emotion. Elliott looked at my father, then at Pearl and cleared his throat. Dad nodded, took the hint like an angel and scooped away a reluctant Pearl, avidly curious, on a pretext of making tea.

Elliott watched the door close, nodded in the direction of the window, listened and smiled. "The child. A fine little chap, I see – and hear. Might we have him in now?" he asked eagerly.

I stared at him in horror. Timmy with his car noises in the garden was being mistaken for Drew's son. "Oh no, no," I said. "That's Timmy. My stepbrother. My little boy – he died."

Elliott MacAeden sat down heavily, suddenly a very old man. His face turned gray, he put a hand to his heart and for a moment, I thought he would collapse. I ran to the door ready to summon Dad.

17

"No, please." He indicated his pocket and I withdrew a box of pills. "Bad heart," he murmured. "Nothing to worry about. Be fine presently."

As he swallowed the pill with a sip of whisky, I knelt by his side. "I'm sorry," I said and he gripped my hand feebly, his eyes full of tears.

"So am I, so am I. Such a shock, after all my hopes. When Rosanna told me that there was a wife – and a son, you've no idea what it meant to me. Drew was everything in the world, the son I never had." He sighed deeply. "It seemed like God's will, giving an old bachelor a child who would inherit Lairigbrach. The line would go on – and on."

Now I understood the terrible reason why he had been quite happy to draw a veil over an unfortunate marriage and a less than heartbroken widow. The child was his only interest in me.

"How – when – did you lose the boy?" he asked, forcing out the words with difficulty.

"It only lived a few hours," I lied, making it easier for him.

I could feel nothing. Nothing any more. Remembering the baby was to relive in minute detail the horrors of that pregnancy, the tortures of Drew and Tony, and the miracle by which I survived to bring Drew's child into the world. I had hoped to die. But I didn't. Despite my ill-usage I was stronger, fitter than I had ever been.

And despite it all, the baby lived. During those first days, looking at his small face, so perfect and so beautifully a replica of Drew's, watching the eyes open in innocent wonder to smile at me, holding the exquisite pearly fists in my hand, how could any mother believe that the child was father to the man and she might well have hatched another monster?

What if my son grew up to be like my husband, in every way? I thought that on the day I left Drew my tortures

18

were over, now I saw they had only just begun. Years, endless years, of waiting, watching for the terrible pattern to emerge, lay ahead of me.

I held him in my arms, loving him because he was small and beautiful and helpless, because he was my flesh-and-blood too. I dropped tears in floods on that tiny face, every time he was brought to me was a long-drawn out agony as I was torn between love, and terror of the evil seed he carried. "Oh, God help me," I prayed.

And perhaps God did. The nurses, then the doctors noticed something was wrong, the baby wasn't thriving as he should. Within a few days the little face wilted, withered like a forlorn but beautiful flower, and then he was gone.

Drew was on tour, I neither knew nor cared where, but some of my friends must have been very busy about notifying him of the baby's arrival.

Weakened, hysterical. I had a complete breakdown and made a fumbling, unsuccessful attempt at suicide. During the treatment that followed even the psychiatrist turned rather pale during our first consultation, or confession (as it seemed to me.)

Then Dad came, gathered up the pieces, said I could have treatment in our home town. At home, Pearl was in the last stages of pregnancy, enormously large, enormously lethargic, insisting that helping with the twins would keep my mind "off things."

Time, beautiful healing time, passed and as I played with Timmy and showered love on him, I thought less often of that other tiny baby, whose infant body had disappeared into Heaven knows what dissecting-rooms and laboratory jars. And I knew that as long as I lived, Timmy would remind me that once I had a baby who was almost his twin.

I told Elliott MacAeden only the basic facts. He nodded vaguely at my breakdown, Drew's disappearance from my life and why I hadn't tried to find him. We were merely cardboard figures in this little drama, but he returned again and again to ask the clinical details about the baby – could death have been avoided, did I think the doctors did everything possible, was it a hereditary or genetic weakness? All these and a dozen other questions.

Pearl tapped on the door, obviously dying for news, and asked if we'd like tea. (Good old Pearl, never had an interruption been better timed). By the time, the tray was on the table, he had, with the aplomb of an ancient lineage, quite recovered his equilibrium.

"How long have you been in Aberdeen? Which newspapers did you take in England?" he asked Dad. "Strange. For years I've been putting frequent requests for MacAedens in all the national newspapers, including that one."

"I never read the personal columns," said Dad, "and besides not being a Scot, the name MacAeden would mean nothing to me. For all I knew it might be a fairly common clan name."

"MacAeden a common name – " For the first time I saw Elliot quiver with indignation. "My dear fellow, it's far from that. Do you know we are the direct descendants of Macbeth."

"The one who had trouble with the witches at Endor?"

He turned to me and for the first time I saw something else in the man's face. The gleam of fanaticism, the touch of madness. It should have warned me that the rest of the family might be tainted with it too. On that afternoon, I realized that "Uncle Elliott" as he insisted I call him, was a collector. Not of butterflies, or stones, but of people – the very unique special, people who were MacAedens. Common sense should also have shown me that with a connoisseur's zeal, the feelings of his human collection would have small account in his plans.

I could see Pearl's eyes widening. "There now," she said regarding me with new interest. "Who ever would have

20

thought that our little Lucy was related to Macbeth? By marriage."

I gave her a cold look, indicating that I might also show signs of Lady Macbeth's murderous characteristics – by marriage. "Little Lucy" I had never been, nor would I tolerate it henceforth.

But henceforth was destined to be short. "How would you like to live at Lairigbrach, Lucinda?" he asked. "Would you permit her, sir?" And before Dad could reply, "I should like to have someone to help me with all my mail and some of the estate matters. Your daughter would seem admirable with all her qualifications."

But it was all a pack of lies. I had recognized the acquisitive gleam. He wanted me among his glass cases, a genuine MacAeden – by marriage.

"And of course," he continued, dragging me further into the net, "Lairigbrach is very beautiful and near town too. You'll be able to come home and visit your little family quite often." He rubbed his hands waiting for my answer and when I hesitated said, "I understand the importers you work for are going out of business shortly."

(Thorough too, I thought.)

Dad said, "Well – " and looked doubtful, but Pearl gave him a none-too-subtle dig in the ribs. "Live out, you mean," she said with a bright smile.

Elliott spread his hands wide. "Yes, of course, Lairigbrach is enormous. Lucinda can have her own suite of rooms, if she cares to."

And I saw my stepmother's mind working. For years and years she had been complaining that this house was far too small. "The twins need a bigger bedroom and Timmy a room to himself. And I haven't a place to put anything." The arrival of TeeDee was the last straw. "That dog takes up too much room." Now at last she saw her dream fulfilled and the workings of her mind were utterly transparent.

21

"Well," said Dad again, "how do you feel about it, love?"

For one tiny fleeting moment, I toyed with the idea of living in the tempting luxury of Lairigbrach. But there was one snag. One irredeemable snag. Lairigbrach had associations, however remote, with Drew. And that was enough for me.

"No," I said firmly. "Thank you, but no."

Elliott's defeat at my decision was purely momentary, his collector's enthusiasm increased by a challenge. From the acquisitive gleam in his eye I suspected he was prepared to haggle over a good bargain.

"I'm not asking you to come for nothing, my dear. I'll offer you more than your present salary, whatever that may be," he added temptingly.

At my side Pearl made eager appreciative noises, willing me into accepting. But I had still one card to play.

"It's complicated," I said sweetly. "You see, I have a dog."

"Is that all?" Elliott's face cleared. "Bring it." He made an expansive gesture. "Bring a dozen dogs, there's plenty of room in Lairigbrach."

For one dizzy moment I saw myself, a civilized Tarzan's mate, leading an enormous tribe of lost and neglected animals along the winding paths of the estate. Even Pearl, never missing a trick, recognized temptation.

"Oh, she'd love Lairigbrach, the little darling," and as if decision was now a foregone conclusion, "I'll just get her." She opened the door and there, sitting in the hall, head on one side like an intelligent actress awaiting her cue, was TeeDee. Ignoring me, she bounded over to the distinguished visitor, all her joy to be measured in furiously wagging tail and a pink tongue centrally situated in the otherwise total darkness of black wool.

"Fancy that," said Pearl, genuinely surprised and gratified. "You see, Lucy, dogs *know*. She likes him, the little pet."

I wasn't cruel enough to add that TeeDee liked all men. They were her one weakness. She accosted total strangers on beach or in park and brought them to me like old friends.

Elliott patted her. Encouraged, she sprang on to the settee and leaned heavily against his side in dizzy-eyed affection, like an aging whore doing the rounds of the pubs on a Saturday night.

In response to my scowl what remained visible of her eyes through the black wool stared contemptuously at a spot above my head, aloof as a dowager at a tinkers' ball.

"Such a lovely nature," said Pearl, selling us heavily to Elliott, an estate agent disposing of a difficult property to a very desirable customer. "Such a tragic wee soul too," she added in hushed tones, "drifting out to sea, she was. Someone had tied her into a shoebox. At Nigg Bay, if it hadn't been for Lucy – but you tell him, dear."

I shook my head. TeeDee's rescue was like my life with Drew. One of those agonizing episodes in life I longed to bury deep enough for oblivion. To forget that cruelty to humans and small animals and birds exists, is enjoyed and goes unpunished, unnoticed. To forget that some rare people have hearts which are purely functional, machines to keep them alive, hearts that have never responded to one gentle, generous impulse in their lives.

Perhaps Elliott noticed my stricken expression for he did not press the point. He looked at his watch, stood up and said, "You're both welcome, most welcome. No, no – please, think it over."

As we waited in the hall, while Dad chatted politely to him, Pearl fumed behind me like a suppressed steam engine, her rage shared by a trapped insect buzzing furiously against the landing window. Nipping my arms

23

painfully, she muttered, "Say you'll *go*. You're mad. Don't be an idiot. Oh, say you'll *go*."

And catching Elliott's eye, she gave him her sweetest smile.

"I'll try to persuade her."

But I would not be persuaded. I could never go to Lairigbrach. Drew was dead, but I had a superstitious terror that anything, however remotely connected with him would bring me misfortune and sorrow.

"Of course we'll meet again," said Elliott.

"I hope so. I'm looking for a job abroad."

"What job?" demanded Pearl sharply.

"In an office," I said, refusing to give details of my still nebulous dream.

Elliott shrugged. "When one is young, travel often seems like the answer to grief. But somehow one never quite escapes, my dear." His searching but tolerant glance indicates that *he* wasn't defeated. This coveted collector's piece, this MacAeden by marriage, might still be accessible.

Timmy, lurking in the garden, rushed over shyly to show the visitor a new car. But with the same remote smile, Elliott brushed the child aside, his eyes bleak and tired.

Small but sensitive beyond his years, Timmy clutched my hand, whispered hoarsely, "Timmy not do nothing." His bad grammar could be forgiven. He was too young to understand the last humiliation he had unwarily inflicted on the laird of Lairigbrach. The agony of seeing hopes dashed as he touched a child who was after all not a MacAeden, the heir he had dreamed about.

Rolling down the car window, he clasped my hand. "I do hope you'll change your mind, Lucinda. I like the feeling of the Clan all living happily together under one roof . . . as they did in earlier centuries."

As he drove off, I waved. I was cold, chilled to my heart by more than a change in the weather. The dark mist on

24

the horizon had grown monstrously. Now it moved inland, throwing a pale shroud over the granite spires and reaching with spectral fingers for the roses in the garden.

The car vanished. Beyond the corner, beyond the winking roadsign "Danger." And I remembered Elliott's parting words:

"Do come, Lucinda. Besides Drew would have been happy knowing we had taken care of you."

As if in echo to his words and my own thoughts about death not being strong enough to contain Drew's evil, the foghorn boomed, close at hand. I shivered, for as I ran up the path and into the house, it sounded remarkably like mocking laughter from the grave.

Chapter 3

That evening in John Knox Avenue promised to be stormy. Outside the fog had crept up to the windows, thickly blanketing the garden. Inside the tiny living room, the atmosphere hung thick with Pearl's dusty clichés about People who didn't Recognize Opportunity when it Knocked on the Door. The TV western was noisier than usual and I could almost taste the gunsmoke. All three children were strident and disposed to be quarrelsome.

Realizing the condition of my nerves, I took refuge at an orchestral concert at the Music Hall, having inherited one solitary ticket earlier in the week from my boss (who was involved in some gloomy details of winding up his business affairs in Glasgow.) If the heatwave had lasted, the idea would have been intolerable, but without hope of escape to quietude at home for several hours, I needed desperately to be elsewhere than the living room which still contained for me the remembered words of Elliott MacAeden and his startling revelations of that afternoon.

I didn't like it. Superstitiously I felt my home contaminated by mention of Drew, as if even oblique reference could magically conjur him back from the grave. Now I understood why in more primitive societies it is taboo to mention one's dead. Sound logic, I thought.

At seven-thirty, with the granite of Aberdeen's Union Street invisible behind chilly mist and the foghorn's wail like a banshee at an Irish wake, I relaxed in the luxury of a second row seat. The musicians assembled, tried a chord. I looked up from my program . . .

And found myself staring into the now hauntingly familiar face of the Barbaric Stranger.

Not behind a guitar this time but in the ranks of the violins.

I blinked furiously, wondering if I was suffering from hallucinations. Then over the loudspeaker came the announcement: "Due to the sudden indisposition of Mr So-and-So, violin, his place has been taken at very short notice by—"

"Hush!" I said to the woman in the next seat. Too late. She stared at me and shrugged, rattling the cellophane on a box of sweets and addressing loud remarks about the weather to her companion. Thwarted once again, I could have hit her. The name had sounded impossible, something like "Eden Atler." It meant nothing to me.

Of the concert, I remember little, apart from that absorbed face above me on the platform. Appropriately enough the program was Sibelius. The Fifth Symphony had never seemed more apt, the moving, haunting, brooding music perfect for the strange feeling of déja vu each encounter with the Barbaric Stranger brought.

Tonight his barbarity was curiously emphasized by evening dress, the discipline of pristine white shirt and bow tie strengthened the power of the face I had once described to Fiona as "an Aztec warrior moving in for the kill." Now, conventionally clad, the present fashion of sideburns added another dimension. The perfect interpretation of a Bronte hero.

Here was Heathcliff and Mr Rochester all rolled into one. Powerful, frighteningly so. Sinister, secret . . .

Who on earth was he?

His presence intrigued someone else in that audience. A pretty brunette in the front row, who obviously knew more than his name, for they exchanged long looks during

27

the interval and smiling, she waggled her fingers at him in a kind of greeting.

Concert over, I lost her as we moved towards the exit. Then in the foyer I saw them talking together and I wondered where this one fitted into his collection of girls. Fiona might consider him ugly but other women obviously found him quite fascinating. Three different encounters and three different girls. It would seem, I thought, he wears them like a wardrobe.

I had to edge past them. He was taller than I had first imagined and as if the sudden furious beating of my heart attracted his attention, he turned and looked at me. In that one exchanged glance, I went out into the night, bemused, absorbed, and in a cheered sort of way I blamed him for my reluctance to go to Lairigbrach. Obviously Fate willed a meeting for us somewhere, sometime in Aberdeen.

On the steps of the Music Hall, I hesitated, considered going back on some pretext to give Fate a chance, a nudge in the right direction. With heart wild, beating at my audacity, I looked inside. The corridor was empty, the time not yet ripe. And as I sat in the bus going home, I felt despair. What competition was carrot-red hair and an undistinguished figure to the voluptuous blondes and brunettes who flocked to his side? And later as I climbed the hill to the council estate, I wondered whether that pristine white shirt and bow tie hid a chain containing a thunderbird around his neck.

That night "I dreamed a deadly dream." I ran, pursued by some unseen horror. In the midst of a strange red desert, a wilderness of rocks. Men on horses. I screamed, awoke, thought the danger was over.

But I wasn't in my bed, but in a dream within a dream. A dark cave. A huge shambling animal blocked the entrance, came towards me, red eyes gleaming. A bear. The scene changed. As a bride I stood before the altar in a small wooden church. The man waiting for me

28

turned . . . Drew's smiling face. I was directing my own horror movie.

Sick with loathing, I cried out. The minister at the altar turned. He had my father's face, but stony, angry, unyielding. I tried to speak to him, explain something, but ignoring me, ignoring Drew's cruel hold on my arms, he went on with the ceremony.

The door behind us crashed open. Another man. Behind him men with painted faces. Screams, shots, confusion. In front of me the minister with my father's face fell, the red rose of death growing, spilling on to the floor. Smoke . . . the angry sound of a wooden building ablaze. I was lifted, carried . . . the wind outside . . . the wind.

As we rode through the night, strong arms held me and I looked into his face. A face I only recognized in dreams. Protector, comforter, lover, mate of my soul. Dark and tired, but tender, loving and infinitely beautiful. Merciful but doomed. "We are both doomed," he said.

"Doomed."

I awoke. Doomed. The word hung in the air around me in this safe, little house on the outskirts of Aberdeen, like the strains of the symphony I had heard earlier that evening. But the face in the dream wasn't the face of the Barbaric Stranger. The only thing they shared was that thunderbird which touched my cheek as he held me against his heart. My cheeks were still wet with tears, even though I knew I had dreamed it all a hundred times before.

Now it was Sunday morning, the sun shone through the window and the twins bounced in. I had slept late and hadn't I promised to take them to the beach? The fog of yesterday had vanished but nightmare clung to me like gossamer threads and I avoided the living room where the atmosphere lay heavy with fragments of remembered conversation with Elliott MacAeden. I shivered. Would I ever feel safe or secure in this house again?

Mention of Drew's name had violated my sanctuary.

29

Now I saw his eyes watchful from every chair, from every picture. I looked at the window curtains apprehensively, sure that they had moved. In a panic that they might spring open to reveal him, waiting, smiling, as he did in dreams.

Oh, why had it happened? Could I never be left alone? To forget. Tired, drained, my legs dragged as the twins and Timmy and my dog, TeeDee, all of them indecently bursting at the seams with energy and gaiety, boarded the bus. Following them upstairs, I felt a hundred years old, exhausted, drained of all life, wondering how I could get through the day ahead, refusing to think of the weeks, months, years of my life, lurking untouched, waiting to be lived. What possible compensation could life offer me for Drew? What believable joys could wipe out the past and its nausea?

As the bus rolled slowly towards town the streets near the city center were bursting with tourists while gay flowered hats with white gloves, indicated churchgoers issuing forth, cleansed in spirit, to go respectably home to safe Sunday dinners and an afternoon of reading newspapers in the garden.

By the time we reached the beach, it had turned into a huge sand-colored canvas, pitted with tiny moving microbes of living color. In the sea, small pinpoints bobbed incessantly, the heads of humans, swimming. Then came the sound, a great rush of noise, the high-pitched drone of the human herd, unleashed, uninhibited, playing on the beach. I wasn't sure that I could bear it at closer range. But the children were already away, three more screaming voices to the throng, beside themselves with delight and excitement, rushing seaward.

I leaned my back against the wall among the sordid remains of packed lunches, ice-cream wrappers, orange peel, and watched them splashing into the sea.

Here I was safe. Safe in a crowd. Danger didn't equate with transistors, laughter, the holiday atmosphere. Danger

30

just wasn't real, I told myself. Then occasionally my head jerked into awareness as a dark head moved in the crowd. But it was never him. My Nemisis, my Barbaric Stranger had for once deserted me, presumably he and his females had better things to do and better places to do them than a Sunday afternoon summer beach.

Still I was disappointed having grown used to meeting him in unexpected places. I wondered if he really existed, or was he some fantastic hallucination, visible only to my eyes. Did some strange disorder of my mind superimpose his face on to any tall, dark man?

Suddenly I longed for Monday, to tell Fiona, to have her tut-tutting, reassuring me that I wasn't mad. I would have run to her that moment like a scared child, had she not been inaccessible in Elgin, visiting Dick's parents, basking in the glory of future daughter-in-law. She told me the visits were agony, but I couldn't quite believe her. Fiona would never have any difficulty persuading parents, even an initially hostile mother, that she was the perfect wife for their son.

In the importer's office where we both worked, all pretense of business had ceased weeks ago. Now the typist's room resembled a fashion designer's studio with pattern books, swatches of material and catalogues of wedding sationery sprouting from every available table and chair. Planning a white wedding was a great occasion and Fiona was enjoying every moment to the full.

But that Monday morning was mine. And her eyes were like cartwheels at the end of the expurgated version of my brief life with Drew.

"You know, I always knew there was something more than a broken romance there," she said triumphantly. "Oh, Lucinda dear, how awful for you. I'm so sorry. About the baby and everything. Yes, I remember reading about that rail crash in the local paper, when you were away in Skye. Great headlines about Last of the MacAedens. But of course, it wouldn't get much coverage in the national press. Such a nice man, Elliot MacAeden . . ."

"Oh, have you met him?"

"Not really. Only seen him at local functions. Fairly popular family, you know." She looked at me apologetically. "Bit mad, of course. Always were, the MacAedens, I mean. Did incredible things."

"What about this MacBeth lark? Is it true?"

"Yes, indeed it is – or so Elliot MacAeden has been trying to prove for years, going great guns that the MacBeth clan had no real connection with King MacBeth but were merely a sept of the original kinsmen. Isn't it exciting?"

"I can't say I'm partial to Macbeth or his Lady."

Fiona chuckled. "Well, well, I'd best be careful, hadn't I. Now that 'out, out, damned spot' means something more to you than taking a dress to the cleaners."

I didn't laugh.

"There must be something in this for you, Lucinda," she continued. "Isn't it super?" And picking up a swatch of materials she held them to her face and peered into the mirror. "I'm so glad, dear, that you've got a lucky break at last. You've been on my conscience, I can tell you. Having to cancel Greece, then the job folding up –"

"Silly, I can take care of myself. But, bless you."

"Will you invite us to Lairigbrach, once you're installed? You won't forget your humble friends, will you?"

"Hold on, hold on. You're well ahead of me."

"How's that?"

"Fiona dear, I'm *not* going to Lairigbrach."

Her mouth dropped open. "Not going. But I hear it's a super place. And such a marvellous opportunity for you."

"For pity's sake, do stop sounding exactly like Pearl. An opportunity for what?"

"To better yourself."

"Oh, come off it. You admit they're a bit mad. The

only opportunity in view, as far as I can see, is to be an addition to an eccentric old man's private zoo of obscure humans."

"Zoo? Obscure humans?"

"Yes. MacAedens. Rare treasures. Freaks, if you like."

"You make it sound as if they have two heads."

"Well, perhaps they have. I wouldn't know, not having met the rest of the family. And before you protest – I don't care to find out."

Fiona was silent for a moment, watching me. "Lucinda. Are you quite sure you're doing the right thing? Think of the advantages."

"There aren't any from my angle."

She groaned. "Honestly, it's not only the MacAedens who are a bit mad, I'm thinking."

"Please, please – don't you start on me. I thought you were my friend. At home, Pearl nags me every minute, dying to get me out of the house, so she can have an extra room. For pity's sake, Fiona. One nag is enough. Besides, I've written away after a couple of jobs. Abroad. One in Italy, another in Spain. Secretary-companion jobs."

A few days earlier, Fiona would have been mad with excitement. Now her gloomy expression didn't change. "Well, I hope you're doing the right thing."

"Now that – *that* was straight from the living room at John Knox Avenue. I had expected more adventurous advice from you."

"I just want you to be happy, Lucinda."

"Well, rest assured of one thing. My happiness doesn't lie at Lairigbrach. Anything connected however remote, with Drew MacAeden could never bring me anything but trouble."

"Oh, for heaven's sake. Forget Drew. He's dead. Dead. Just think – "

"No, no, NO. I won't think. I refuse to be cajoled, bullied or otherwise beaten into submission. I'm not going to Lairigbrach. And that is most finally, *that*. Now, if you don't mind a change of subject, I intend having a quick lunch and then the library, to study the jobs being advertised in the literary mags."

"I suppose you see yourself as secretary in some exotic clime, finding romance the way it happens in all those serials you read," said Fiona nastily. "Believe me, dear, you'll only end up with some nasty bald-headed writer who'll make a pass at you, or some dreary old woman who is neurotic. And they'll all bully you – "

"Of course they won't – "

"Of course they will. Because you, dear," she said, poking me with a sharp fingernail to emphasize the words, "because you are a *natural* to be bullied."

"And what does that mean?"

Fiona blushed. "Well, Dick says – I mean, we both think you're the sort of girl who makes tyrants. You're just too – vulnerable, you listen to everyone's sob story, never believe anyone could be telling you a lie. And taking people on good faith, you expect love and kindness from all the world in return." She sighed. "Lucinda, dear, you never seem to learn that there's a cruel, sharp world outside."

"I learn. I am learning. I have learned." And rather sharply I seized my handbag and went out for coffee. Fiona followed me and we sat rather uncomfortably eyeing each other across the table, throwing out small talk with frantic urgency. As though it was of the greatest, most world-shattering importance, whether I got tights to match my new dress or my shoes.

Two weeks passed. With them the chances of those exotic jobs abroad. With alarming alacrity, which proved my temerity in applying for situations in exotic climes: qualifications, an over-sized ego and under-sized talents, I received polite little notes, thanking me for my interest, but that the vacancy had been filled.

34

Fiona made wry faces, but breathed a sigh of relief. "It's all for the best, I'm sure," she said, indicating that I wasn't the sort of creature to be trusted out in the wild wood without a keeper. "You'll be better off in Aberdeen," she added. For Aberdeen, read Lairigbrach, I thought, with Fiona betting heavily on the side of the Laird of the MacAedens.

Even Pearl was resigned to my continued presence in her coveted extra bedroom and we settled into our normal domestic bickering, almost as if Elliot MacAeden had never happened. The Barbaric Stranger and the weird nightmare had both disappeared from my orbit, so with the heatwave gone and all the signs set for summer, medium boring, I had just washed my hair that Friday evening, when the phone rang.

Pearl shouted upstairs, "It's for you, Lucy." And when I rushed down towelling my hair, she whispered, her eyes gleaming with excitement:

"It's a man. From Lairigbrach."

Sick, trembling, I listened to the voice. "Mrs Drew MacAeden? I'm afraid I have some rather bad news. Mr Elliot MacAeden had a heart attack a couple of weeks ago. He's back from the hospital, a little better now and has particularly asked to see you. I wonder if it would be possible for you to come to Lairigbrach this weekend."

My heart thumped wildly. I was sure it was clearly audible at the other end of the line. "You mean, to stay? For the weekend?"

"That was the idea." The voice was deep, rather amused and extremely attractive. I wondered what the face that went with it was like, remembering radio announcers and seductive tones that so often revealed disappointing faces when they appeared on television. This, I imagined, would be no exception. Kilted, mustached, gray and fifty, I thought.

He was apologizing. He would have collected me but

had to wait for a business phone call from abroad for Elliot. Could I possibly take a taxi? I said I would come right away.

When I told Pearl, who was breathing down my neck, she beamed and squeezed my arm in the smug fashion of one whom destiny has singled out for benign and particular interest. I saw the pictures flashing through her head as she sat on the bed and watched me pack. Pictures of what my bedroom would look like with new wallpaper, paint, furniture.

She was even prepared to make a fuss over Tee-Dee, whose tail wagged politely but in whose eyes lurked faint disbelief. "I'll take care of you, won't I, pet? Until Lucy gets settled. Oh, you'll love a great big house with a lovely garden to play in. It's just what little dogs need," she added slyly, studying my reactions.

The thought of taking a taxi to Lairigbrach when it was quite accessible by bus appalled me by its reckless extravagance. It would be wildly expensive and I hadn't been brought up to ride hither and thither in taxis. Such luxuries were reserved for weddings, funerals and late night emergency drives to the maternity hospital. The whole idea seemed monstrously ostentatious.

So without mentioning the transport suggestion to Pearl (who would have called me an "absolute fool, when they're paying for it") we set off to the bus stop. Pearl was dying to tell Dad the news.

"I'll meet him off the Edinburgh train tomorrow – that's what I'll do." (And take him to every decorators shop in Aberdeen on the way home, I thought.) "Just like him to have a meeting and miss all the excitement."

She gave me an affectionate kiss. For those moments while we waited for the bus to arrive, standing arm-in-arm, smiling happily at each other, we presented a close approximation to the picture of devotion my

36

acquaintances fondly imagined between stepmother and daughter separated by little more than a decade in years.

Half-an-hour later, on another bus speeding along Great Western Road, I decided it was rather sad we could only be friends in absence – when Pearl thought she was getting rid of me. But of course, she wasn't. I had no intention of staying at Lairigbrach. We sped through the suburbs. In a turmoil of uncertainties, brooding on my thoughts, for some idiotic reason I got off the bus too soon.

I was at Lairigbrach, but at the wrong entrance. There were lodge gates, locked and a cottage inside, deserted. I could see nothing of the house. One needed to be on top of the bus to catch even a glimpse of its chimneys. Everything was hidden from the road, secret, private. The world locked outside.

Furiously, I stamped down the road, and the rain began.

A car shot past. Hooted and stopped.

Someone wanting directions, no doubt. Just his luck to pick the one person in Aberdeen who can even get lost between bus stops.

The door opened. "Hello, Lucinda. Thought I recognized you," he said, with an amused glance at my bright hair, which added: Once seen, never forgotten.

"How nice to see you," I lied, wondering who he was.

Offered a lift, I said I was going to Lairigbrach.

"Great, hop in. There's a mile of drive. And you're at the wrong gate. No, no. You're not taking me out of my way. I have a patient there. That's where I'm heading."

The word "patient" registered, although the ordinary, pleasant face under the deer-stalker hat hadn't done so. He was one of Fiona's young men. Hamish. Hamish Faro. My heart pounded madly. Of course, of course, Dick's predecessor. Who knew the Barbaric Stranger.

Now, at last, all would be revealed . . . A simple question.

But I couldn't get in a word sideways. He drove slowly, full of questions about Fiona. Where was she, what was she doing, he asked, using the drive shamelessly to get imformation about her.

When I told him she was engaged and getting married soon, his convulsive jerk at the wheel and surprised, "No!" swiftly gave way to silence, and a depression that was quite tangible.

I watched his gloomy face with compassion and said, "It was all very sudden." I felt apologetic about it.

"It was indeed," he said and gave me a suspicious glance, as if I had somehow contributed to Fiona's change of heart.

How did one explain that Fiona, naturally kind-hearted, never had the wit to tell any of her men that this was The End? Instead she used evasiveness, delaying tactics, promises of future meetings vaguely distant. How could I explain to this poor fellow that Fiona had a cautionary streak? She didn't care to waste any man who might come in useful some day, so that a year in her life became a clutter of untidy ends and some very confused men. I never quite understood how she managed it.

Before I had a chance to satisfy my curiosity about his friend who played the guitar, the violin (and a field of luscious females), the dark rhododendron drive parted and through a sweep of lawns, there was Lairigbrach.

Lairigbrach. And not one bit what I had expected, this sprawling rather ugly Victorian house, which looked as if it had been thrown together by a bad-tempered architect with an unpopular client, a stern budget and an inadequate deadline. The only stab at grandeur, a couple of unhappy Gothic pepperpot turrets stuck on the gables. I had expected a real-live Scottish castle, like Crathes or Muchalls, graceful and mellow. Disappointed and unimpressed, I noticed the date 1856 above the door.

Hamish gave me an encouraging smile and rang the bell.

For a moment I thought there was no one at home and was glad I didn't have a taxi ticking away behind me, awaiting payment. Then the door swung open.

"Boss is expecting you. Go right ahead. You know the way, Hamish." The voice was rich and deep. I recognized it from the telephone call earlier that evening. It belonged to the face of the last person on earth I had expected to open the door to me . . .

I was ushered into the Lairigbrach by the Barbaric Stranger himself.

Chapter 4

"The Boss is expecting you . . ."

So the mystery was solved. My Barbaric Stranger was a servant in Lairigbrach who spent his spare time as a musician in order to support a string of females. Or was it the other way round – a musician maintaining an expensive hobby by working for Elliot MacAeden?

His elegance and informality suggested valet would be the appropriate role, I thought, following him into the house. Then he turned and smiled, that slow, curiously radiant smile which broke up the savage planes of a face which conceded nothing to curves. Now, at closer range I understood why he had such appeal for the ladies – a smile, wide-spaced, dark eyes and a mouth which would have been a sculptor's dream. All were gentle, but their compassion took nothing from the essential forceful male.

I noticed too how beautifully he walked. As a rather clumsy girl prone to despatch glasses of sherry to upholstered and carpeted graves at parties, or to choke on a cup of tea or spill the contents of my handbag on genteel social occasions, I have a built-in envy for built-in grace. And grace the Barbaric Stranger certainly had. But again like the gentleness of eyes and mouth, this grace was male and strong and extremely sexy.

Yes, I thought. The very word might have been made for him. A sexy servant. And I had a mad desire to giggle. The set up was getting more like the "Marriage of Figaro" than "Macbeth."

In the dark hall of Lairigbrach, ashen faces peered uncertainly from gloomy portraits and a decor of some-what self-conscious Scots bric-a-brac. Deer heads, clay-mores, targes and a small artillery of ballistics covered every square foot of wall. There was even a suit of armor and a tattered battle flag. Presumably all must have been herded in from the former Castle as no one in their right senses would have decorated a Victorian hall as if a state of seige were imminent.

A magnificent carved oak staircase yawned towards the upper floors. A river of blinding sunshine shattered the gloom, as the dark hall was invaded by light from the large drawing room on the right, cosily furnished in the pleasanter aspects of Victoriana. Faded olive green velvets and a scarlet Persian carpet, muted by time to gentle marigold. Against unobtrusive walls, rosewood furniture and on one wall a splendid tapestry.

It depicted a battle scene, presumably Macbeth in an anachronism of tartan plaids and eighteenth-century gear. A huge solar window through which the sun shone so vigorously, overlooked lawns, trees and beyond a ribbon of silver twisted away to the west. The River Dee, and on the horizon the Hill of Fayre drowned in gathering sunset clouds.

The view was magnificent. I said so and he agreed.

"A drink? Sherry?" Handing it to me, he said, "I'm Eden, by the way. I expect the Boss has told you all about me."

Before I could say no, the telephone rang in the hall. While he left me alone to answer it, I discovered my first illusions of magnificence about this room were beginning to wilt a little. As I looked around, instinct said this was a sad house. Sad despite its airs of grandeur . . . it had been built on foundations of sorrow . . .

I shook myself. What a ridiculous and unbidden thought. Again I was morbidly aware of being hypersensitive about houses. Ever since early childhood, I had been aware of this "feeling" for houses, finding their atmosphere as revealing as a human face. As if all the joys and sorrows of their occupants throughout the years somehow were absorbed into the woodwork and plaster to remain there, a living brooding force as long as the building survived.

It took no effort on my part to understand the condition of haunted houses, although I never wanted to experience a "haunting" or to have any of the present fashionable ESP experiences.

But this house . . . I had known from the moment I set foot in the sombre hall. Built on sorrow, bitterness, its walls ached with tears, its bricks were agony. It was frightening to feel such power emanating from the stones around me.

"Sorry to be so long," said Eden, pouring himself a drink from the whisky decanter. My eyes widened, he was fairly liberal with Lairigbrach's hospitality. He flung himself gracefully into a chair and sat eyeing me narrowly, and I suspected rather more appreciatively than befits servant and guest.

"So you're Lucinda MacAeden. Well, well." His lingering gaze was amused and slightly insolent, that of a man for whom womankind held no more mysteries. And I knew with a sense of electric shock that this first meeting was disaster. He didn't find me remotely attractive. Worse, he didn't like me. I knew that . . . and with a shiver of fear, I recognized too that this man and I could very easily become enemies.

He moved suddenly, I jumped and as usual some of my sherry slopped over my fingers. Patting them dry with a hanky, I wondered what on earth *did* I expect? Suddenly indignant, I wondered why I was letting a servant intimidate me, when I was a guest in Lairigbrach.

Afraid of this stranger, afraid of a house which brooded like a sullen, jealous woman, I remembered Fiona's remark about breeding tyrants. For once I saw what she had in mind. I was the meat that martyrs were made of.

Eden wandered to the fireplace and consulted his watch. He was nervous, too, ill-at-ease. There were footsteps on the stairs and he again said, "Excuse me."

In the hall I heard him talking to Hamish and would have done much at that moment to summon enough courage to rush out and beg that pleasant, homely young man for a lift back along the Deeside Road.

A murmured conversation, an exchange of goodnights. Eden returned, consulted his watch again and said, "I'm terribly sorry about this. Hamish says the Boss is under sedation and won't be able to see you until tomorrow. Alison promised to be back. But she's involved with an exhibition and there are complications." He looked at me hopefully and I nodded vaguely wondering who Alison was and wishing he didn't presume that as Drew's widow I knew them all.

He smiled patiently, obviously waiting to be dismissed.

"If you have an appointment, please don't let me stop you. I'll be perfectly all right, if you'll just show me to my room."

And there again was that oddly dazzling smile. Gratitude had worked wonders. "How kind," he said, almost whisking me up the wide dark stairs, in case I should suffer a sudden change of mind. "You see," he explained, "I have a date and, well, it's rather awkward. She –"

"Please don't apologize," I said hastily. "I'll be quite all right." (Heavens, I didn't want the story of *his* love life.)

"Sure?" he asked with the politest of frowns. "Alison should be back very soon," he added encouragingly. Outside a door on the dark landing, he paused. "That's the Boss's room. He has a resident nurse, so if you want anything, she knows the run of the house." He pointed to the opposite door, threw it open and said, "This is yours. Like it?"

I had walked in cautiously expecting the worst and was enchanted. "How lovely," I said.

"The decor hasn't been changed since the house was built. It's more than a hundred years old."

The original blue brocade hangings on the walls, and the canopied bed had faded into a strange mist of color, the carpet too where pattern here and there had retreated into invisibility. There was a massive rosewood wardrobe, ready to absorb crinolines and full-skirted coats and a marble-topped table complete with mirror and an old fashioned toilet set of ornate jug, basins, soap-dish.

The whole effect was utterly charming. And to complete the picture in a marble fireplace supported by chilly white cherubs, a coal fire glowed. More than anything else in the world, the prospect of falling asleep in warm firelight delighted my twentieth-century soul. For I was a flat-dweller born and bred to a world of smokeless zones where open coal fires were taboo and council houses centrally heated with clinical efficiency.

But the old cry of "decadence," of knees singed and a frozen back didn't bother me. All my life I had nourished secret yearnings for the romantic, old-fashioned cheer of a *real* fire. And in a bedroom too. What luxury.

I wished I could share my excitement with someone. But not this young man, eager to depart from my presence.

"Everything all right? Bathroom's through there. Great," and putting down my case, he gave me a happy smile and rushed downstairs. A moment later I heard the front door close, a car door slam and the screech of brakes where the drive turned sharply. Whatever his faults, he didn't keep 'em waiting.

I sniffed the air. This room smelt different from the rest of the house. Old wood, polish, lavender, patchouli, herbs – the ghosts of perfumes whose fragrance was lost, long ago, but which had clung through the years to brocades and curtains. It now conjured up scenes of dressing for the

Ball, of Christmas morning and new-born babies crying in the depths of the canopied bed.

The room was wonderfully, excitingly alive, long after the hosts of its departed occupants had crumbled into dust.

Awareness of the past and awareness of eyes watching me. Eyes from a portrait whose smiling face dominated the room. A girl with ringletted red hair, darker than my own, an off-the-shoulder gown, and in the extreme right-hand corner of the portrait, another picture, the turreted charming sixteenth-century castle whose foundations had provided the site for the "new" house.

The girl held a book in her hand and marked the place with a coral rhododendron bloom, from the drive which blossomed behind her. A glimpse of formal garden, a Mercat Cross, the shapes of distant cottages, a crumbling Gothic tower.

Through the window I saw the background of the portrait still existed. It had been painted from this very angle and the time of year was now. A summer scene, with all the light and shade in the garden appropriate to this hour of the evening.

And I realized as if she breathed at my side, that this had been the bedroom of the girl in the painting. This same scene but oddly distorted by time. For time had been busy outside.

All traces of the formal garden, except for a tree still recognizable here, an overgrown shrub there, had vanished long since. And as though some forgotten holocaust had removed all trace of the distant cottages, only the Mercat Cross remained leaning at a drunken angle among sour bracken that had swamped the garden. Only the fragment of Gothic ruin, allegedly Macbeth's hunting-tower had survived, lacking merely a few more stones to show the passing of yet another century.

I looked again. Apart from the sad deterioration in the

world outside, it was as if the girl had dressed in Victorian clothes and posed for the painter. Uncannily, as if someone had rolled away time like a carpet of lawn to that other summer.

"Janet MacAeden, b. 1850—" The date of death had been omitted. It worried me. I wondered why and smiled back at her as if she could see me across the years. On the mantelpiece, in a copper bowl, someone had placed a solitary coral bloom, identical to the one she held. A gentle sentimental touch, I thought, and quite out of keeping from what I expected of the hard-headed inhabitants of Lairigbrach, who were reckoned to be from vague testimonies of Fiona and Hamish, "A bit mad."

I went through the door Eden had indicated as bathroom and found it situated down a couple of steps in one of the turrets, perhaps a dressing room in the earlier days. There was nothing Victorian about the elegant pink suite, a white carpet and, on a hot rail, warmed towels waited.

How comforting and welcoming, I thought. Clearly the rooms had been carefully prepared for an important visitor. As it could only be me, I tested the water, found it hot and plentiful and decided to enjoy the kind of leisurely bath John Knox Avenue never provided.

Baths at home were skimpy affairs, the electricity used to heat water constantly surveyed, deplored and begrudged. Always Pearl's warning, "Don't use all the water. Remember the twins and Timmy are to bathe as well." Only pre-school children and babies had a daily bath.

As I lay in scented luxury I decided I was going to enjoy my weekend at Lairigbrach. Meeting new people always intrigued me. I had a sneaking suspicion I'd like to write A Book someday. How wonderful to capture the atmosphere and set its background in this house. My literary yearnings I still kept to myself, they were too nebulous, too delicate to stand the harsh light of day and of friends' laughter.

Besides the time wasn't yet, when it was, I would know. Meanwhile I prepared myself mentally by absorbing and observing, hoarding personalities and places with the cannibalistic manners and vigor of a sea-anemone.

Filling the bath until it reached my chin, I rehearsed my speech about Lairigbrach to Pearl and hoped I could show her my "rooms" someday. Giving way to an excusable vanity, I felt just a little gloating about how impressed she would be.

Switching off the light, I returned to the bedroom, feeling very good indeed. From bath salts, soap to matching cologne, talc and perfume, all very expensive indeed, someone had a very good idea of what a humble working-girl craved for in the way of luxury. At that moment, it didn't seem like an elaborate confidence trick or a splendid piece of emotional blackmail, this touch of the fairy godmother's wand.

Which was exactly what someone intended I should think, someone who knew how to tempt luxuriously.

The trap was baited. The spring in place.

I was to be my own executioner.

Chapter 5

There is no real darkness in a midsummer Scottish night and I was too stimulated ever to sleep in that great canopied bed. I tried experimentally closing my eyes, but always opened them to find Janet MacAeden smiling, apparently watching me with some curiosity.

Finally I put on my housecoat and sat on the window seat. The house was utterly silent, except for occasional movement in the corridor, soft-footed firm footsteps as the nurse attended to her patient in the bedroom across from mine. It must be late. I wondered if sometime I had dozed and missed Alison's return. Should I go downstairs and look for her? I thought better of that. She would be tired, wanting to go to her bed, hardly an opportune moment to introduce myself.

But there was another reason for my reluctance to move. If I spoke to anyone, the spell would be broken. I would destroy the magic web – the atmosphere this strange room, haunted by the smile of a girl long dead, was weaving. I let it absorb me, becoming part of a kind of waking dream, no longer striving or concerned to maintain a separate identity . . .

Time passed and outside strange birds called over the river. Once in the garden below an owl killed its prey and announced the fact in weary jaded triumph, "Wooooo-oo-oo, woo-oo-oo." A distant night-jar's echoing cry hurtled across the sky and was lost. Night deepened, took on the rich cobalt blue of a stage set for romantic ballet, the curtain newly-risen on "Swan Lake."

Hugging my knees, utterly content, I waited. And the eyes of the portrait watched me, approvingly, it seemed. I had made a new discovery and I smiled back at her. Now I knew why I had been so restless in John Knox Avenue, so impatient in Feather Court, Newcastle. Now I saw that all the threads of my life, my sinews and tissues, my moments of hope and desire, had been pulling invisibly waiting for someone – or some *thing* to tie them together. To give a purpose, a reason for my life.

And now I had come home. For a brief timeless hour, I had touched the ultimate happiness. In Janet MacAeden's room, where I had come at last to a sense of belonging. This moment had been waiting for me all my life and even Drew's obscure connections, the agony I had lived with him had been but a single step on the way.

"Drew." I whispered the word. Bolder I said it out loud. "Drew." But for the first time there was no warning shiver, no twitch of horror. Drew was dead. He could never again harm me. I was on the way to being healed, made whole and clean again.

From the bedside table I took the jug of milk so obligingly left, beside an old-fashioned wooden biscuit barrel. I filled a glass, held it up to the portrait of Janet. "Thank you," I said. "Thank you."

The milk tasted delicious. A prosaic glass of milk, which I didn't care about normally. This was sweeter, different, a new taste. Perhaps milk could change to nectar in the magic of this room.

I returned to my window, nibbling a digestive biscuit, sad that the magic hadn't extended to the biscuit barrel. As I settled again on the window seat, for one of those infinitely rare moments, I understood the meaning of pure contentment. I felt an affinity with this house, with the sleeping garden and the whole world growing dark and secret outside.

With it came recognition that whatever lay ahead, I would rest content, not to fight against the tide but to go with the ebb and flow of life. Content not to wish my life were different, the past unwritten, the future known, but content to ride on the tide.

As if a small invisible thread linked me to the whole universe, I was aware of something that men might call God – stronger, more infinite, more perfect and controlled than man's feverish longings, his struggling frustrations and anguish. I had reached out and touched the meaning, the divinity of human life. Deep inside me, beyond words, the question had been asked of me and I had given the correct answer. I had looked with my blind eyeless soul and seen the wheels of the world at work.

I had seen "where past things are and Who cleft the devil's foot." I had seen the stars made and how the world began. And I would never be able to write, or tell a word of it.

Already it was disappearing. Outside the trees stirred warningly, their sleep disturbed as a shaft of bright light swept along the drive.

Someone had come home.

Striving to recapture my mood, I ignored the light touch on the door. It was repeated. I became fully aware. Clocks ticked, time was back in business. I moved over to the door and the little gossamer thread that bound me to infinite joy, to the truth and meaning of life was suddenly broken and gone. Forever.

Resentfully I opened the door. Eden came in, carrying a tray.

"I saw the light," he said. (Fool that I had been not to turn out the lamp at the bedside.) "I thought as Alison hasn't come back, you might be starved. Like some coffee?"

Back in the world, I knew that milk would taste of milk again and had a sudden yearning for coffee. "I would. It smells delicious."

Eden smiled. "Sorry about Alison. Her exhibition opens next week and I'm afraid she's rather disorganized at the best of times."

I wondered who then, if not a woman, had been responsible for preparing this room for my elaborate reception?

"Are you quite comfortable here?"

"Very. Thank you," I sipped my coffee, found it delicious.

"Didn't wake you, did I?"

"No. I couldn't sleep. I was sitting by the window."

"Really. Are you sure?" he asked.

"Of course I'm sure." I wished he would stop asking questions, while I tried, an unequal spider, to recapture my lost gossamer thread.

"You look like someone who is just back from a long journey. You know, not quite re-orientated yet."

"I never left this room," I said indignantly, wondering if he thought I'd been snooping about and making free with the silver.

"Oh, yes, I believe you." His eyes touched the copper bowl, briefly met those of Janet MacAeden. "But there are longer journeys than leaving this room. The journeys of the mind. Do you remember at school, 'How many miles to Babylon, Three score and ten'?" He paused.

"'Can I get there by candlelight? – '"

"'Yes, and back again.'" And he looked at me then for the first time with approval. I retreated under that penetrating glance, embarrassed that I should give so much of myself away to a stranger.

Perhaps it was some sort of trick. Perhaps he had seen me watching him at our earlier encounters before we met at Lairigbrach for the first time. Had he seen my admiration, the attraction I felt towards him at that dance with Fiona, or at the concert? Or did some strange chemistry between

51

us make him aware of things that it would have been kinder to discreetly hide?

In which case it would be wiser not to be added to *his* collection. Elliott collected MacAedens, Eden collected females. The thought amused me. I hid a smile by yawning and let my eyelids droop in pretense of weariness. "What time is it?"

"One o'clock. We don't keep late hours at Lairigbrach. Besides my girl lives in the Hall of Residence, she has to be in at midnight."

His girl. My girl, he called her. Ah, there had been wisdom in discreet hiding. This man was just too devastating and I hated to think of the consequences of revealing attraction, or whatever it was. I suspected him of alchemy, that he might take what one offered and use it for his own purposes. I wondered if the girl was the brunette I had seen lingering in the foyer with him on the night of the concert. Were they engaged or having an affair? Was it serious this time? Was she The One?

As if he knew my thoughts, he smiled, daring me to ask.

"I think we've met before," I said hastily. "At a dance. Hamish was interested in a friend of mine, Fiona . . ."

He frowned, shook his head. "Sorry, *have* we met?" His searching look showed embarrassment too. "I don't recall –"

How flattering, I thought, that he remembers nothing of those encounters. Dance, party, concert. Carrot-red hair can't be so conspicuous after all, I told myself, winning consolation out of humiliation.

"This is such a lovely room," I said.

"Isn't it just?"

"Was it *her* room?"

"I thought you knew."

"She's lovely."

He looked pleased. "She likes you too." A log broke

52

and threw a shower of sparks up the chimney. "Don't look surprised. It's always warm in this room when she likes someone. There's also a saying in the house that she only really smiles for those she loves."

He regarded me head on side. "You're rather alike. Both with red hair. And the way it grows, to a peak on your foreheads. A widow's peak, isn't it called?" He stopped suddenly embarrassed, obviously remembering that I was newly widowed.

"Yes," I said quickly. "I'm glad she likes me."

"Look at her now, eager, waiting."

"That's just an illusion of the flames flickering," I said and we both laughed.

"I've been wondering when she died. Why there's no date."

"Don't you know the story? Good heavens, I thought all MacAedens dined out on this one from the age of ten." He took off his jacket, threw it over a chair. "Mind if I make myself at home?"

Even on a warm night like this, he was wearing a polo-necked sweater, very hairy and Shetland, the kind one suspects is worn more for penance than pleasure. Yet he gave it, as he would give all clothes, a kind of barbaric dignity and grace.

"You were asking when she died. No one knows for certain. It's a fascinating story. Her father was a younger MacAeden son who went into the church, a failing of younger sons of the aristocracy in those days, who were offered church or army if they wouldn't inherit the title.

"So David MacAeden had enormous energy and missionary zeal. In those days of empire-building it was very much in vogue to sponsor a lost cause of one's own discovery. Lost causes were natural to the MacAedens and as there were no wars current, he decided to spread the fiery cross and convert the heathen.

"Top-ranking heathens at this time were the American

53

Indians, regarded as badly in need of the white man's mastery by bullets, starvation, annihiliation – or conversion.

"So David MacAeden departed on an evangelical bent. He went to California, where his own kind were scrabbling about cutting each other's throats for gold. In the Sierra Nevada, the white man's god was called Gold. David MacAeden built a life for himself, a church and a house and when he considered the time was ripe he sent for his wife and the girl Janet – soon after this painting was made. She was then about seventeen.

"Her mother, Mary, died in childbirth of a still-born son the following year, long after David and she had given up all hope of having another child and David had already adopted a son, one of the local Indians, Atala, who was the young chief of the Atalos tribe.

"Unfortunately Mary MacAeden was the chronicler of the family and afterwards only rumor drifted across the Atlantic and found its way to Lairigbrach. But what rumor –

"Chief Atala, after years of devotion to his foster-father, who bestowed on him an expensive university education and all the benefits that he would have bestowed on a genuine MacAeden, turned savage again. He murdered David MacAeden, abducted Janet. There was one hell of a massacre and after that – only rumor continued to filter through.

"There were reports of Atala and Janet being seen in various states. It would have been easy for Atala to assimilate into what then passed for white civilization in the west, where a man was never asked for his real name but only, 'What name are you traveling under?' Atala spoke perfect English, was trained as a lawyer and the Atalos weren't even as red-skinned as most Mexicans.

"Rumor reported two children, left with friends in Tuscon. Some say Atala and Janet were murdered by Apaches and died together in the Arizona desert. But as late as the thirties they were reported as being seen in San Francisco."

"But Janet would be nearly ninety then."

"And Atala nearly one hundred and ten." Eden smiled. "However as Atala was considered by the Indians as the representative of the Sun God on earth, he was also supposed to have the secret of eternal life. So perhaps it wasn't such a strange story after all."

"Do you believe it?"

Again Eden smiled. "Perhaps it was just a popular legend. In youth they must have made a striking pair, a redheaded woman and an Atalos Indian who was over six feet tall, and a legend even in his own lifetime. But I don't suppose you've heard of him."

"But I have. Weren't the Atalos the subject of a great controversy? Didn't someone try to prove they were descendants of the Atlantans, who had migrated to the West Coast of America, when the continent of Atlantis was destroyed?"

"A tricky voyage by sea in those days, and no mistake. Another Kon-Tiki, with a vengeance."

"What happened then?"

"They eventually settled in the Sierra Nevada mountains and were cut off by an earthquake – they had chosen a nice little refuge straight on the San Andreas fault – this earthquake was before the Conquistadores and cut them off completely from the rest of California. So they missed not only the Spaniards but the early pioneers – until someone rediscovered them. It was even rumored that they were the inspiration for Conan Doyle's *Lost World*, and a dozen other such yarns."

"Yes, I remember seeing it all in an epic western called *Beyond These Blue Mountains*. I've seen Atala in other films too."

"He was almost as popular as Geronimo, Cochise and Sequoya at one time. But he wasn't at all like any actor who

55

ever played him in a movie. Seen any painting of him? No? I have one around somewhere. It was made by a gold miner in 1864 when he was about thirty."

"I'd love to see it." I looked at Janet again. She wasn't smiling. Or had the shifting firelight turned her expression into something sad and wistful, as if she too remembered with Eden. "Poor Janet."

Eden shrugged. "What about poor Atala, who lost his birthright all for one woman?"

"What about the woman? It wasn't her fault, being carried off by a savage Indian?"

For a moment, Eden said nothing. Then he smiled, a faint mocking smile. "Come, come," he said smoothly, "I'm sure it wasn't as bad as all that for Janet. You're rather influenced by seeing too many movies of Apaches descending on blazing wagons in glorious technicolor, aren't you?"

I shivered. "It was probably a lot worse than that, than anything we've ever seen."

"But that, my dear girl, didn't only happen in the American West. That is precisely the story of the Border Raiders, and of the Scottish Clans. Kill, burn, rape. Remember Montrose and the Sack of Aberdeen? Besides, the Victorians had such a dull time, probably rape was the secret dream of the females of the time, under all those vapors and false gentility. I imagine she was every bit as shrewd as her modern equivalent."

I gave him a hard look, wondering if he thought I was in Lairigbrach this weekend for what I could get out of a sick old man. But his expression was innocent. I felt angry suddenly at this male ego, this cynicism. The belief that women were cattle, mindless creatures suitable only for breeding or amusement. Somehow I hadn't expected it from him. It seemed completely out of character.

"Believe what you will," I said, "but I can't imagine a

civilized cultured woman like Janet MacAeden *enjoying* being abducted by a savage like Atala."

Eden turned from the picture, leaned one elbow on the mantelpiece and said lazily, "Interesting. Some day you must teach me a little more exactly what you mean by 'savage'."

"It doesn't bear thinking about."

"Does it not, indeed? How sensitive you are." His voice was cool, mocking and the slow smile had something dangerous in it. I remembered my first impression that this man and I might one day be enemies and regretted having asked him to sit and chat over a cup of coffee in my bedroom at one in the morning. I decided on a swift change of subject, to less explosive topics.

"Who put the flower there beside her?" I asked. "And how did you come to work for Elliott MacAeden? What, in fact, do you work at here?"

Eden drained his coffee cup, placed it on the tray. "The answer to your first question is that I put the flower there. The answer to your second question is no, I am not an employee of Elliott MacAeden. I thought you knew who I was or I would have made the situation clear earlier and saved you embarrassment. As a matter of fact, I'm a relative – a kind of umpteenth cousin.

"The MacAedens aren't the only ones to boast of royal lineage, even if it was to a blackguard and a murderer. Atala was considered by a whole race as the direct descendant of the Sun God on Earth – like the Pope in Rome."

He picked up the tray and went to the door. "The reason, Lucinda MacAeden, that I put flowers beside Janet as long as they bloom in Lairigbrach, is that I can't put them on her grave. No one knows where she lies. I have a soft spot for the lady in question. Your savage Atala and Janet were my great-grandparents.

"Goodnight, sweet dreams," he said and closed the door softly behind him.

Chapter 6

"Savage." The word hung in the air. Small wonder, for I realized I had used it with embarrassing frequency. And from the portrait Janet's eyes smiled, perhaps now with a touch of mockery.

Savage. Had she thought of Atala as a savage, or did that not matter once she fell in love with him? I shuddered at my lack of intuition about Eden. I should have known. There was no excuse for me especially as first impressions had suggested an Aztec warrior. He certainly had the features of an American Indian, but he was very tall and slim and no darker than the Mediterranean races. (I discovered later that I had a considerable amount to learn about so-called "Red" Indians.)

Eden Atala. I should have known. I could only take refuge in ignorance, that one does not normally expect to find a genuine American Indian living in the suburbs of Aberdeen, related to the local laird, and the end-product of two ancient races so wildly different: the great-grandson of legendary Chief Atala and the alleged descendant of King Macbeth.

"Savage" whispered the pillow as I turned my head and tried to sleep in vain. How on earth could I face him again? I rehearsed speeches, discarded them and finally gave way to the grossest cowardice. I should just avoid him as much as possible. Exhausted by my mental gymnastics, I fell into a troubled sleep.

Next morning, as I went downstairs, from the kitchen

issued voices. The deep and now familiar one of Eden, and a breathy giggly female voice. Both were raised in cheery goodbyes and after what sounded suspiciously like a smacking kiss and another delighted giggle, the back door closed.

I waited, heard the car noisily depart and opened the kitchen door. I expected to find a young girl, a maid perhaps, but the girlish voice belonged to a sturdy middle-aged nurse in crisply starched uniform. She was in sole possession of a massively bleak kitchen, which had been despondently modernized some thirty years ago. Now paint-peeled doors and walls revealed a pock-marking of browns and dismal greens, all that remained of earlier transformations.

"I'm Nurse Duncan," she said. "I've made a pot of tea, there's toast and porridge." She spoke rapidly, that young girl's voice at variance with a firmly corseted figure, strong arms and legs and short graying hair.

"My patient's awake now – oh yes, fairly comfortable, thank you. He's asked me to send the young lady to see him as soon as possible. That'll be you? Aye, he should have stayed in the hospital much longer, but as you'll gather, he's a very obstinate man. Very." As she spoke, she thrust out an elbow, consulted her watch sternly, as if I was standing waiting with a thermometer in my mouth and a pulse to be taken.

"Actually," she continued. "They're a funny lot in this house, I think. I mean there's money but not much evidence of it being spent on the house." Her eyes traveled the shabby walls. "Artists and such-like too, and the place drooping for a bit o' paint. Well, you can keep these houses with character, as they call them. Give me ma wee flat in Ashgrove." Again the watch was consulted. "Here it is, coming up for nine o'clock and Miss Grantly not risen yet. Artists – " she gazed heavenwards and pursed her lips in extreme disapproval.

59

Miss Grantly. Alison. Alison Grantly. Now I knew who she was. A local painter whose work, vital and full of color, I had often admired in exhibitions.

"Is she one of the family?" I asked eagerly.

Nurse Duncan gave me an old-fashioned look. "Well, not officially. But she's more right to Lairigbrach than anyone here, if truth were told. Wrong side of the blanket, poor lass – "

Above our heads an ancient bell jangled. "That'll be for you, lass. No rest for the wicked, eh? By the way, I didn't get your name, Miss –?"

"Not miss. Mrs – MacAeden. I'm – the widow of Drew, who died recently."

"Oh, oh," she said in a shocked voice. "I never knew. Nobody told me. I understood Mr Drew was a bachelor. Oh really, and there I was – " she blushed trying to remember what confidences she had passed on to me. "I never knew you were one of the family, especially you not knowing about Miss Grantly and all," she added reproachfully.

I put a hand on her arm. "Don't feel badly about it. I'm ashamed to say I enjoyed listening. You see, I'm a stranger here too. I've never met any of them before either. My marriage to Drew was – well, secret."

"A secret marriage. Oh, how lovely and romantic," she said and as I followed her upstairs, she whispered, "All right. I forgive you," and ushered me into the master bedroom. A large dark, over-powering and supremely ugly room, as only Victoriana at its worst could ever achieve. From every corner loomed solemn mahogany furniture, old but lacking the grace one expects of antiques, with none of the gentle beauty, the wistful elegance of Janet's room.

I lingered by the door as Nurse Duncan saw to her patient's comfort and announced my arrival. "Don't over-tax him," she whispered as she left us.

60

Panicking, I longed to rush after her, and continue an absorbing and informative conversation about the MacAedens over another cup of tea. Today I had more than my usual dread of sick visiting. There are lucky people blessed with wonderful bedside manners, who can cheer up invalids, make them laugh and feel good. But alas, I am not one of them. Nervousness makes me extra clumsy too and I sit carefully, rigidly, afraid that some sudden movement will send the fruit bowl spinning, or knock the thermometer on to the floor.

The sickroom puts a terrible pall over me and I approach invalids speechlessly and hospitals with terror. All humanity, all natural cheer drained away by the solemnity of bedpans, charts and clinical whiteness.

As I walked across the room to where Elliott MacAeden lay, sunshine streamed through the window catching in its rays the dust of a hundred years, dust from inaccessible corners and carvings turned to dancing specks of gold. Sunshine showed up something else too. The man in the bed was dying. I saw with pity, too, that he was a stranger, changed out of all recognition.

Perhaps he would not even remember me, for we had talked for only a short time at John Knox Avenue. Like a coward, I hoped this would be so, then I could flee downstairs, back to the solid world of the living, to toast and tea and Nurse Duncan's confidences. Closing the door on the shadow of death, like this sunlight for ever drawing nearer, nearer to the wax-colored face in the bed . . .

Looking down on that face, banality, hypocritical smiles and false heartiness sounded like sacrilege. How could one ask, "Feeling better?" or "You're looking well", in the face of this monstrous take-over bid, this transition from one world to the next.

He saw me and smiled. "Ah, my dear," he whispered, "so you've changed your mind and come to Lairigbrach after all." (Presumably no one had told him I was here

61

on a weekend visit only.) "Have they given you Janet's room?"

When I said yes, he patted my hand.

"Good, good. She'll like that. She'll like that."

And I wondered for one awful moment if he were so far gone that he had already established communication with the world of ghosts, of the dear departed. I took his frail hand. The skeletal bones, the whitness, the blue veins. Suddenly I felt ashamed of being young and strong and foolish, while this man who was good, kind and useful had reached the end of a worthwhile life. If I could then have given him ten years of my ineffectual, broken life, I would cheerfully have done so.

He noticed my woeful expression and said, "Don't look sad, Lucinda. There isn't much time. I've known about this day of reckoning for years. Not all heart, my dear. Other complications too. They told me years ago there was no hope so I've been living on borrowed time. I'm quite reconciled, I've made my peace and I'm ready to go when the call comes. So let's forget about that and talk of something much more interesting."

He smiled. "My dear, there's so much I want to know about you and Drew. So much," he sighed. "Drew was like a son to me, the son I never had. I'm not saying he was faultless, that you shouldn't have left him. I know he was wayward, stubborn, and a thousand other things. But I worshipped that boy, there was nothing in Lairigbrach, or this world too good for my Drew." He looked at me approvingly.

"And I like you, Lucinda. I approve of his choice of wife. I knew the moment we met that we would be friends. Actually, Drew had me worried for a while. He knew some odd folk and used to bring them here until I objected. Some of the ladies – ah well, young folk will be young and different, but they weren't what I was hoping for as the future Mistress of Lairigbrach. Now tell me, how did you two meet?"

"It was when we lived in Newcastle, before Dad's move to Aberdeen. Drew was playing at the theatre and we had a party afterwards for the actors at the community center – "

"How romantic." (Romantic said Nurse Duncan, romantic said Elliott.) And romantic was an ill-chosen word, considering what followed. I thrust back the loathing of remembrance. Nothing could have been further from romance. Oh, I fell in love, I don't deny, as every woman who ever met Drew did. I was rapturous, unbelieving that he could possibly love someone as insignificant and ordinary as me. When marriage wasn't mentioned, I told myself I was being foolish to expect it, after all weren't we thoroughly modern. Who wanted ties to all eternity, vows, marriage?

Two and a half months later, I did – and badly. I was also determined I was not going to be talked out of having the baby. Much to my amazement Drew in reply to my letter, dashed through from Leeds that Sunday and said, of course, we must get married.

He seemed pleased about the baby. Obviously my instinctive doubts, suspicions had been wrong. Obviously he loved me more than I had thought. I was content. If he loved me, nothing else mattered. I wouldn't question my good fortune by asking why? With Drew I could weather any storm and proudly.

I didn't know then that the pleasure he was getting out of this situation was a unique revenge on Tony. It seemed a drastic way to end one of their many quarrels, to make Tony (who was the better actor of the two) suffer for having departed to a small part in a New York stage production, while Drew toured the provinces with the third or fourth company.

"Go on," said Elliott. I hadn't said a word to him.

I didn't know where to begin to search for something redeeming, something human to say which would delight this poor, deluded, dying man. Again reluctance was mistaken for embarrassment.

He chuckled thinly. "I understand. But as I told you before women always found Drew irresistible. Even plain old girls like Alison. She's touching forty and mad about him. You should see her when he's around. Now that surprises you, doesn't it?" He patted my hand and I smiled, not bothering to tell him Alison and I had not yet met.

He cleared his throat in an apologetic manner, the sound reminding me of our first meeting in the living room at John Knox Avenue. My safe happy secure little home. It seemed like something from another world, with only Pearl's outbursts of bad-temper to contend with. Safe and happy world, I watched it retreating already a million miles beyond the stars . . .

"Don't be ashamed of the shotgun marriage, my dear. In part I was to blame. You see, I used to go on at Drew about getting married. Thirty nearly, I'd say, time you stopped fooling around and got yourself an heir. An heir for Lairigbrach.

"During the last few years, there were so many overseas tours, Australia and so forth, that he didn't come often to Lairigbrach. Just a hasty weekend from London or Edinburgh during the Festival. Once, when we were having supper together he said, 'I'm not the marrying type, Uncle, the state of matrimony doesn't appeal somehow, but I just might do it. To give you your heir for Lairigbrach. As a small repayment. It would also oust Rosanna. You'd like that too, you old dog, wouldn't you. She'd never get her hands on this house, if I had a son.' Then he smiled and slapped me on the back. 'Well, Uncle, it's nice to know that if I get some girl pregnant, you won't be shocked and outraged.'"

"When did he tell you this?"

64

"Nearly four years ago. The last time we met," he said sadly.

"Nearly four years ago". And with that remark drained away the last of my self-respect. I hadn't only been unloved by Drew from the very beginning, I had merely been a brood mare, a vehicle to please his uncle and assure his own future by providing an heir for Lairigbrach.

I wasn't listening to Elliott going on about Drew any more. Sickened, I turned my head away and the sunshine mocked me. Everywhere I went it seemed, I now found something more about Drew, something more to undermine my pride. Even that lover's night in which the baby was conceived was premeditated, calculated, as everything else in Drew's life.

Knowing him had been like throwing a stone into the center of a still pool. The ripples grew and grew, wider, wider. I shivered, thinking it remarkable that even death could put an end permanently to his mischief, and destroy the apparent ease with which he had manipulated other people's lives.

"A severe shock that day. If only the child had lived, Lairigbrach would have been his. Yes, Lucinda, when you told me he had died, that was my death blow – "

I hadn't been listening to a word. Now outside a car drove up and stopped. A door closed. Elliott stirred peevishly against the pillows.

"What a noise, what a noise. That'll be Eden. You've met, of course. I hope he was polite to you. Oh, good. A very surly, unpredictable young man, I'm afraid, but quite good at heart."

He sighed. "We all make mistakes in our time, my dear. And sometimes I feel I'm not quite as shrewd as my business dealings would have me believe. I think Eden was the greatest mistake I ever made, bringing him here to Lairigbrach, in the vain hope that we could prove he was one of the family, a MacAeden. Now after ten years or

65

more of throwing money down the drain, it turns out he's just a fake after all."

"A fake?"

"He's not a genuine MacAeden."

I stared at him, hardly able to believe my ears. This collector of humans, who dismissed a man with the same lack of emotion as he would have thrown away a costly stamp he had found out was quite worthless, regretting only his expenditure and fervently hoping that the "fake MacAeden" had not tainted his whole collection."

"Of course, he's clever. Talented, musical – many of these hybrids are."

"Hybrids?" It was fantastic. He talked as if Eden were some sort of butterfly or insect.

"Yes, indeed." Elliott sounded irritable again. "He was reared by Indians but he obviously has a large percentage of white blood. He's never done one thing to please me. He could have made a career of music. That I would have appreciated – " (And, I thought the vicarious glory of a famous MacAeden) "– But what did he choose? Science, if you please," he added in tones of disgust.

"Scientists are up and coming these days, very respectable," I said consolingly.

"Respectable, but so dull. He couldn't even choose something spectacular, a heart-transplant man, a space scientist – those I could have forgiven. But what does he choose? Plants. Growing plants. A sort of glorified gardener, it seems to me. Then I discover he has this idiotic idea of growing plants, so that he can return some day to this fool reservation where he lived as a child and make it self-supporting."

"Reservation?" I asked.

"Yes, some damned scruffy Indian reservation in Arizona. He was glad enough to leave it as a boy, now he sees himself as the saviour of his people, leading the modern-day Indians to victory. Taking over where his great-grandfather, Atala, failed. Chief Eden Atala. I ask you!" he laughed bitterly. "No consideration for me, no feeling for Lairigbrach. And if I don't do something about it before I die, he'll sell us all down the river." He stopped, looked at me and smiled.

"That's why I'm so glad to have your help, Lucinda. You and me, we won't let him win, will we? We'll save Lairigbrach between us." He listened for a moment. "Who's outside there? Go and see."

For a dying man he had sharp ears, I thought, certain too that I had heard a movement outside the door. I opened it but the corridor was empty. How odd, who would want to eavesdrop?

"Probably Nurse Duncan," I said, "she told me not to weary you."

"Old fool," he muttered. "You're the best thing that's happened to me since my Drew died. Drew knew what Eden was. They never got on together even as boys. Drew knew he was a fake right from the start and it was such a disappointment. I had such hopes of having a splendid time with my two boys, of being father by proxy. Drew used to come often those days in the summer vacation, whenever Rosanna could spare him. And Eden would be like a stag at bay, primitive enough still, despite his civilized manner, he was already defending his territory.

"Tell me, did you ever meet Rosanna? No? I'm not really surprised. Drew was her nephew, she'd brought him back from Australia on one of her visits, the Melbourne branch of the family, you know, and adopted him when his parents died. Rosanna was quite beautiful when she was young. At one time, we were engaged to be married – "

A gentle rap on the door and Nurse Duncan came in. "What, are you still here, Mrs MacAeden? I said five minutes, not half an hour. Off you go now and let my patient get some rest. Really, Mr MacAeden, you are naughty." She took his wrist firmly.

"You old gorgon," he whispered, "I asked her to stay."

"She can come back later. You be quiet and stop arguing." And with a quick frown she dismissed me.

In the drawing room I found a sluggish fire, lit several hours earlier and hanging on to life by one glowing log which would shortly fall into ashes. I wondered who had prepared the fire?

Was it the same mysterious hand that had prepared my bedroom? There was no sign of a servant and I hardly imagined Nurse Duncan did domestic chores as well as looking after Elliott.

For the first time, this magical appearance of fires and welcoming touches for a guest, like the hot towels, the careful preparation of the bathroom the night before, struck me as faintly sinister. Once long ago I had seen a reissue of Cocteau's fantasy film, "La Belle et La Bete." In this house it seemed, there were strange echoes of that castle where invisible servants attended to Beauty's needs, with cups filled and tables laid by unseen hands. And arms shot out of walls, holding lit sconces to guide her on her dark way.

In the mirror above the mantelpiece, a great gilt affair, spotted with age, I caught sight of my face. Tired, plain. The carrot-red hair too bright, too heavy for the white face in which the eyes were dark hollows.

Certainly I was no Beauty, but the Beast might well lurk somewhere.

"By the pricking of my thumbs, something wicked this way comes." Aptly enough from Macbeth, I thought, deciding that I must walk warily. Unlike the fairly tale, I had no thought that my Beast would turn into a handsome prince. There would be no happy ending in this tale for me, I suspected as I poked the fire, which needed more than magic to keep it going in a room turned suddenly cold.

I wondered whether there was something more than being "a bit mad," i.e. eccentric, about the MacAedens, as Fiona had hinted. Was there something rotten at the very core?

First there was Drew's corruption, then Elliott, who sought to add MacAedens like butterflies to his human collection. Surely there was something more than eccentricity there too?

If "blood would out," then there must be a place for Alison. And Rosanna, whoever she was, a MacAeden who had once been engaged to Elliott. And Eden too, perhaps? A member of the family by adoption, had some of their taint rubbed off on him? Had he been the listener outside the door? What had he been hoping to hear? When Elliott died shortly, what secret plans had Eden made to "defend his territory?"

In the fireplace, the log exploded in a shower of sparks. Unused to open fires, there was something frightening about its violence, the sudden roar, the smell of wood burning.

I shivered, the feeling that began in Janet's room last night, the sense of the familiar, was creeping up my spine again . . .

Behind me the door opened. I turned blinded by the flow of sunlight streaming through the window. All I could distinguish was a tall figure, a pale face, fair hair. A light shirt, trousers . . .

For a moment I was paralyzed with terror, then as I sprang to my feet, the poker crashed noisily to the floor.

The dark outline of the figure in the doorway . . .

Drew.

Chapter 7

"I see you're making yourself at home."

The figure moved into the light, took shape, became female. "Alison Grantly. You must be Lucinda."

Her handshake was firm, her rather staccato voice deep. In appearance she completely shattered the gentle ethereal image I had attributed to Alison Grantly. Large feet in mannish shoes showed evidence of many muddy encounters. Those strong masculine-looking nicotine-stained hands had built the exquisitely dainty water-colors which I had so often admired in art shops. She wore MacAeden tartan slacks, ancient in age rather than lineage. As those were predominantly rust-colored, the shocking pink cardigan she now pulled on (home-knitted, sadly bagged at elbow and bottom,) did scant justice to slacks or lavender shirt. The short crisply curling hair would have been striking, had it not sadly lacked a recent shampoo. Certainly the sensitivity for color had apparently quite exhausted itself in the journey from easel to personal wardrobe, and sadly I concluded the mystique I expected from and associated with artists was missing.

Bastard or no, her eyes were MacAeden. Drew, Elliott and now Alison. Put a long curly wig on any of them and one would get a surprising resemblance to Charles the Second.

"Sorry I wasn't here to welcome you. Seen Elliott yet? Have they made you comfortable? How did you think he was looking? Had any breakfast?" All these questions were machine-gunned at me, without waiting for replies, as she took up the mail, thumbed through it and seized one letter, throwing the rest down in an untidy heap.

She read it through with an exclamation of annoyance. "The old bitch."

The doorbell rang and she disappeared to usher in an elderly man in black, severe of countenance, accompanied by a younger man in black, still nervously an apprentice in expressions of severity. Both carried briefcases, one antique, one new. "Will you wait in here, please," said Alison.

"Just papers for Mr MacAeden to sign," said the elder one. He nodded in my direction. "Perhaps this young lady could oblige by witnessing his signature. Not a member of the family, of course." His hearty laugh changed into an embarrassed cough as Alison said, "She is, I'm afraid. But there's a nurse upstairs – "

Twittering laughter outside announced Nurse Duncan, closely followed by the silent-footed Eden. She gave him an adoring look and rather high in the countenance, led the two men upstairs.

Despite all my intentions, I was face-to-face with Eden. This morning Chief Atala's great-grandson lacked only feathers and war-paint and hair a couple of inches longer. I felt myself blushing all over again for my tactless remarks about "savages" last night. How could I ever have been such an idiot? I took refuge in a polite smile and gazed at the window. I need not have worried, he ignored my presence, busily exchanging meaningful glances with Alison.

"You realise what the Boss is up to?" he asked her.

"Of course I do. Here, read this." And Alison handed him the letter. "What do you think of that? The old bitch," she repeated.

Eden sighed. "I don't see what we can do to stop her if she wants to come. She is MacAeden after all. And we're not officially," he said bitterly.

71

"Old vulture. She's just coming for pickings."

Perhaps the mention of vultures and pickings reminded Eden of my presence. He turned his dark brooding gaze on me. "As you're likely to be around for a while, Lucinda, we had better put you in the picture. You might as well be prepared for Rosanna."

"When is she coming?"

"Tomorrow."

"Then I'll miss her." I intended to. Rosanna as Drew's adoring aunt was the one person I could happily miss. "I have to be back to work on Monday, and er – I have things to do at home."

Eden smiled. "Not any more, you don't.

The letter he took from his pocket read: "My dear Elliott, I was sorry to hear from Eden of your continued illness. Most interesting to know that our Miss Lucinda Hetton is connected with the MacAeden family. In view of this and the imminent closing of our Aberdeen branch, I shall of course be delighted to release her services to you immediately – " It was signed by my late employer, who seemed indecently eager to be rid of me.

"And what exactly does this mean?"

"It means that you've been transferred to the team. Welcome aboard or whatever they say in such circumstances. You now have the privilege of working for the Boss, like Alison and me. If you finish reading the letter you'll discover the melancholy arrangement 'as long as you need her services.' You realize of course, that he is a dying man. Don't look so indignant, cheer up, you'll soon be released."

I gave him a furious look. Did he have to imply that I was an absolute hound, begrudging a dying man his whim.

"But what is there for me to do?"

"Don't worry. I'll find plenty to keep you busy. You can take over some of the domestic duties from Alison for a start, until her exhibition is over. I'm also led to understand that you're an efficient secretary. So you can help me sort out the Boss's tangle of administrative affairs. Unfortunately typing and writing letters aren't my accomplishments."

"But what about Rosanna?" asked Alison impatiently. "I won't be here much next week."

"I think I'll be able to manage Rosanna single-handed," said Eden grimly and I wondered for a moment if he had a tomahawk tucked away somewhere.

"Why did she choose this particular time? Elliott asked that Drew's body be buried in the MacAeden vault and she didn't even come to the funeral."

"She was supposed to have the flu, as I remember. Well, perhaps as she missed one family occasion, she's decided to be in plenty of time for the next."

"Really, Eden," said Alison, sounding shocked.

"Really, Alison. Don't let's delude ourselves that family affection motivates Rosanna. Or any of the other sudden arrivals in this little drama." He looked at me insolently. "Probably she wants to take a look at the opposition."

"Opposition?" I asked.

"Of course. I expect you've heard by now that Alison and I are not genuine specimens of the MacAeden clan. When your husband died the only runner-up for the Lairigbrach stakes was Rosanna. However, it looks as though she's now to be supplanted by Drew's widow – "

"Why? I'm not a MacAeden."

Eden smiled without mirth. "Drew was Elliott's blue-eyed boy and he has his reasons for not liking Rosanna. So he's prepared to cheat a bit and consider you are a genuine MacAeden – by marriage."

"There's no need to be brutal about it," said Alison severely.

"Oh, for God's sake, Alison, let's cut out the hypocrisy. We all know exactly why Lucinda has been brought here. We all know exactly why Rosanna has been on the telephone twice a week since the Boss's heart attack. None of it alas, due to blood being thicker than water." He turned to me. "I'm sorry if you think I'm being brutal, but it's a corny situation after all. Don't you think so?"

"Why should I?"

"Come now, you can't be all that innocent. Surely you read books or go to the movies? Haven't you seen a hundred stories with all the family gathered in a spooky old house waiting for the last of the line to die, all hating each other, all suspicious, wondering who will inherit?" He laughed. "All we need is a murder or two thrown in and we'd have the perfect setting for a vintage Agatha Christie – "

"Eden," said Alison in shocked tones. "Don't be so beastly."

But Eden ignored her as he watched me steadily. "I haven't shocked Lucinda though, despite all her innocence. I haven't even frightened her with the possibilities. She's got strong nerves," he added thoughtfully. "Well, not to worry, you aren't really depriving us – I'm only joking. Neither Alison nor I want or need Lairigbrach – "

"Indeed no," said Alison. "I don't want it. I just stay here to please Uncle Elliott as an unpaid housekeeper. Work damned hard too and not even appreciated. I'd be tons happier with a flat in town."

"There now, Lucinda. And I don't want it either. I never did. I have my own plans for the future and Lairigbrach doesn't fit my scene at all. I'm only here because the Boss needs me as general factotum, which duty I perform free and gratis, because he brought me up by hand," said Eden.

"That's fine," I said. "As far as I'm concerned then, Rosanna can have Lairigbrach and I'll be on my way. Nobody consulted me or my feelings in the first place. If you really both want to know, I never wanted to come to Lairigbrach. Despite your genius for implying the worst possible motives I only came out of kindness to a sick man.

"Rosanna doesn't need Lairigbrach either," interrupted Eden flatly. "But I gather she could never let anything go past her. She's probably on the lookout for antiques for her overseas customers."

"The old bitch," said Alison angrily. "She buys antiques here for a song, then takes them to Australia and fairly feathers her nest with the proceeds. Rank dishonest, I call it. Oh, you haven't met her, Eden. Wait till you do. A trouble maker, plain and simple."

"There's nothing plain or simple about trouble makers, Alison."

"I only met her once. Twenty years ago. I expect she's changed a lot since then, and none of it for the better, either. All I remember was this typical ex-chorus girl, a blowsy peroxide blonde. Very vulgar. And very grasping."

This surprised me into saying, "Elliott said they were once engaged."

"Engaged, my foot," Alison snorted. "She tried to trap that innocent deluded creature into marrying her – "

There were footsteps outside the door. Eden stood up. "Continue your story. I'll see the gentlemen off."

I had a feeling he left the scene with some relief, that he had heard this story many times before and that it bored him. I suspected that I too, bored him.

"Fancy you not having met Rosanna. She brought your Drew up, you know," said Alison reproachfully, as if the lack of contact was somehow my fault. "She absolutely adored him and spoilt him rotten." She looked at me quizzically. "I suppose she thoroughly disapproved of him marrying. She was that sort of person. No girl would be good enough for him. Now where was I?"

"Rosanna and Elliott. They were engaged." I was

amazed. A blonde chorus girl was the last possible choice I would have hazarded for an intellectual, persnickety man like Elliott.

"Oh, yes. Rosanna was over from Australia with her parents for a holiday. They were MacAeden cousins who had migrated. Oh, they were both young then. Anyway, I think she wangled a proposal out of Elliott when he was drunk or something and then he regretted it. But before he could change his mind, she had put out all the wedding invitations. Naturally Elliott was cross, considered he should have been consulted in the matter. The next thing, she had flounced off in high dudgeon, threatening breach of promise and revenge. Then we heard, she had set herself up in a remote Dorset village, like a spiteful latter-day Miss Haversham, with an antique shop.

"Then the only MacAeden cousin left in Melbourne died and Drew was left an orphan. She adopted him, encouraged him to become an actor and when he wasn't on tour, they worked this antique business between them.

"But Elliott says she never forgave him. All through the years she has been plotting how to get her revenge and lay hands on Lairigbrach, which was obviously the reason she wanted to marry him. Drew tried to put matters right between them and for a while they have exchanged Christmas cards and she sends him caustic postcards from abroad on her eternal gallivantings about the world."

The telephone rang and Alison went to answer it.

Suddenly the wrangle over Lairigbrach was no longer sinister, just sad, pathetic. I thought of the time and useless energy wasted by Elliott striving to add to the MacAeden human collection, and wondered as he lay peacefully dying if he had any regrets. I went over to the window and suddenly I wanted to be away from them all, wandering around the grounds in the sunshine, over tempting lawns to the glowing river beyond the trees. I'd sit on a stone and dabble my feet in the water and listen to its hypnotic gurgling. Then when a shadow fell across the sun turning the water cold, I'd put on my shoes and scramble through the bracken and explore Macbeth's secret tower, then the Mercat Cross . . .

But it was not to be. It seemed we were in for a day of visitors. Hamish was next, to see his patient. Afterwards he came downstairs searching for Eden or Alison, who had both seized the opportunity to escape and leave me in charge of the kitchen. I was preparing a list of groceries, having delighted Alison by promising to vaguely "look after things." I was also aware that Eden's cloak of general factotum might have been specially tailored for my own shoulders.

"I hear you're staying," said Hamish, putting down his bag and taking a cup of coffee. He shook his head. "A miserable business but I'm afraid there's little time left. Nothing dramatic, he'll just slip quietly away. Thank God for pain-killing drugs these days. We can do that much for him. With his present deterioration, it might be just hours now."

He gave me an encouraging smile. "It's jolly good of you to stay around and help them out. They need it, believe you me. Alison and Eden, they work like trojans. Always have."

I didn't feel like spoiling his admiration by saying that a gun was being held at my head.

"So the bad Rosanna is coming too. What's she like? Oh, you haven't met? Quite a character, I believe." Obligingly he drained his cup, rinsed and dried it. "By the way, I'm going into Aberdeen. Anything I can get for you?"

"Not really, thanks. I can phone this list to the grocer. Oh, I wonder – would you put me on to the bus route though? I really ought to go home and collect some more things and see my small dog."

Hamish grinned. "I'll do better than that. I'll wait and bring you back."

When I telephoned Pearl, they were rushing off to take the children on a promised picnic to Balmeddie. They were also taking both dogs.

"If," Pearl asked slyly, "you're not wanting to take TeeDee back to Lairigbrach."

"Hardly worth it for a couple more days," I lied.

An hour later with a suitcase packed and waiting in the hall at John Knox Avenue, I felt the sharp sting of apprehension at leaving this calm safe haven. It *was* just a feeling, outrageous, absurd, that danger loomed ahead. As Pearl had remarked "nobody could have been nicer or more considerate to you in Lairigbrach," but without any basis in fact, the sense of danger remained, uncomfortable and persistent.

I wondered if the day would ever return when this pleasant cozy living room would cease to affect me like the scene of a fatal accident I had witnessed, where each time I passed by I would remember the sprawled bodies, the blood on the road. Every time I opened this door, over and over I saw Elliott sitting on the settee, drinking sherry, and bringing Drew, dead but restless, back into my life.

Now the settee was occupied by Hamish, drinking tea and talking what Fiona called "a blue streak." Hamish was never at a loss for words.

All that was required of me was to listen, to smile encouragingly, nod yea or nay. Climbing stories, camping-abroad stories, student stories – each one reminded Hamish of another – an endless stream of amusing monologue and vivid travelogue.

A gifted entertainer (who might well have chosen another profession than medicine, although his bedside manner was assured of success), he was never boring. In addition to being amusing, he had the advantage of being very attractive to look at. Fair wavy hair, gray eyes, aquiline good looks indicating ancestors among the

78

marauding Vikings who raided the north-east coast with such ferocity long ago.

Now I wondered if at first meeting he had not been smitten with Fiona and had showed me marked attentions instead, would I perhaps have fallen in love with him? Suddenly I wished I could put back the clock, rush into that past and believe that my destiny was cast with a man like Hamish Faro.

As we closed the door of the council house behind us and he carried my case to the car, I thought too how such a situation would have delighted my family. Especially Pearl, who was addicted to doctor-nurse romances and television hospitals and approved of all medicals as potential husband-material. A dignified profession, yet accessible to "ordinary girls" who worked in shops or offices.

"This is my day off," said Hamish. "There's a film at the Odeon. Like to come – "

"Love to," I said eagerly, perhaps too eagerly.

An exciting Western, we emerged blinking at the daylight at eight-thirty. Hamish held my arm lightly and I noticed the admiring glances he received from the girls in the queue.

As we drove off he said, "Enjoy it?"

"Very much. But the Indians didn't remind me of Eden."

He smiled. "What do you expect? That Eden would be going around with feathers in his hair? He's a long way from Arizona now."

"How did he land up in Lairigbrach?"

"Good Lord, you don't know? I thought everyone had heard that story."

"Well, I didn't. Nobody tells me anything."

Hamish grinned. "Well, it was like this. The Boss, as Eden calls him was on a lecture tour years ago in the States. Afterwards a man came up and asked if MacAeden was a common Scottish name, because he had fought in the South Pacific with a Navajo Indian by the unlikely name of Atala MacAeden. The American, Riley, had been a Marine officer and some of the Navajos had been trained as a communications team. By transmitting in the Navajo language, they gave and received messages in a code the Japs couldn't break, so there was no loss of time for coding and decoding involved.

"The Navajo MacAeden saved Riley's life under fire, they became friends and when MacAeden was killed by a sniper's bullet, Riley promised to bring up his small boy, then living on an Indian reservation in Arizona. When the war was over Riley intended to go for the boy, but he lived in Washington, he was married with several children of his own and they were having a hard time financially, so his wife wasn't exactly thrilled at the prospect of another mouth to feed, particularly an orphaned Red Indian boy.

"Elliott dashed off to Arizona and after several months of searching in vain, he eventually found a boy of fourteen, Chief Eden Atala, leader of the few Atalos Indians who remained. He claimed to be descendant of Chief Atala and Janet, the daughter of the Scots minister, MacAeden. However, there were no documents to support this theory, to prove as Elliott insisted, in chapter and verse the boy's identity. Still he couldn't afford to leave such a valuable prize behind, so he brought him home and has, I understand, spent a fortune since trying to prove that Eden is genuinely a MacAeden – "

The car swung into the lodge gates of Lairigbrach and down the dark drive. The house looked bleak and unviting for the sun had long since vanished behind the Deeside Hills. Now the countryside lay flat, oddly contourless as it slept, like a landscape from a bad painting.

Hamish switched off the engine and looked at the house thoughtfully. "Sometimes I wonder if it's all been worth it. What is Elliott trying to prove? Rumor would have it that all that was decent and noble in the MacAedens departed with David MacAeden when he chose the church so long ago. Since then an evil, a corruption, perhaps even a taint of madness seems to have crept in. There are some fine tales abroad of past days, I can tell you." Suddenly he stopped, looked at me. "Don't let any of it rub off on you, Lucinda. And don't underestimate Eden, either. Try to like him. He's not so strange really. Great-grandson of a legendary hero of the Wild West, his own father a World War II hero. It's a lot to live up to. In addition to being a good scientist, I'm told, he has the courage of a lion. And he's a damned fine fellow," he added defensively.

Suddenly he grinned. "You know my trouble, I talk too much. Anyway, I've enjoyed today. We must do it again, have a meal sometime. Perhaps we could make up a foursome with Eden and Gillian – "

Which was Gillian, I wondered?

"I think it's marvelous the way you're coping with Lairigbrach. They're darned lucky to have you." He escorted me up the steps, turned the door handle. "Don't bother to knock. Just walk in. Everyone else does," he whispered and squeezing my hand, he kissed me very gently good night.

I watched him spring into the car, thinking how pleasant it was to be appreciated and also surprised and delighted by that kiss. Perhaps I had already established one friendship at Lairigbrach with the breath of permanence about it.

But even as the thought came, there was no flickering answer from within. My heart remained obstinately silent, unstirred, unimpressed. And I waved goodnight, despairing that this numbness inside was to be the story of my life hereafter. It made nonsense of my pretence that I could fall in love again, even with a man as attractive as Dr Hamish Faro.

Chapter 8

As I walked through the hall there were voices in the drawing-room. One of them an octave higher than normal, was painfully familiar. I opened the door and there was my stepmother Pearl drinking sherry with Eden. Judging by the high condition of her complexion it was one of several.

She gave me a triumphant greeting. Curiosity rewarded she had descended on Lairigbrach. As I responded to her affectionate display (especially for Eden's benefit) I was lost in admiration for her audacity, wondering how even she could explain to herself the effrontery of bulldozing her way uninvited into a house whose owner lay dying upstairs.

I wasn't long in suspense. My arrival was the signal for a small bundle of jet black wool to catapult into my arms, while a small pink felt tongue licked my face in a frenzy of delight.

The delight was mutual. Hugging her, I forgot annoyance, realizing only how much I missed TeeDee. Pearl was clever. She recognized TeeDee as the weak link in my armor.

"Oh, she was so sad without you," she pouted, "the little darling. Hardly eating a thing." Even writing off eighty percent of the statement as Pearl's tendency to gross exaggeration, I was still ashamed of neglect. "I just had to bring her. Especially as we were passing the door – "

"I thought you were going to Balmeddie for your picnic."

Pearl gave me a reproachful look. "There was a cold wind off the sea. It was bringing Timmy's earache back, so we went inland to the Forest of Birse instead. You would have thought TeeDee knew where you were, Lucy. She started going mad with excitement when we were coming home. Just before Cults – "

I didn't feel like stating the obvious. That TeeDee's telepathic powers must be truly remarkable as at that time I wasn't in Lairigbrach at all, but at the cinema with Hamish.

"So I thought I'd bring her for a little look at you – "

And yourself for a little look at the set-up, I added silently. Pearl's intentions were glaringly transparent. Eden looked amused. Suddenly ashamed of my family, I saw he wasn't fooled by her nosiness. Probably if she hadn't been so young and pretty with her curls and coy glances, her lovely mini-skirted legs, he wouldn't have given her houseroom, I concluded uncharitably.

"And, of course, we knew your uncle had invited her, so that would be all right. He took quite a fancy to her. 'Be sure and bring her,' he said. And er – Eden," she gave him a long sexy look, "Eden says she won't be a nuisance."

Eden merely smiled, offered her a cigarette and refilled her sherry glass. She looked at me anxiously, bothered by my silence, the nearest Pearl would achieve in remorse. "You see," she began weakly, "it was like this – "

"Yes, yes, Pearl. It's fine, really it is. You did the right thing. It's lovely having her with me," I said, nuzzling my cheek into warm, dark wool and being amply rewarded by great sighs and extravagant kisses.

"This is a super house," said Pearl, relaxed at last, sipping her sherry and preparing to enjoy herself. "Aren't you lucky to live in such a lovely place? That view of the river too. Just like being in the heart of the country."

"Yes, isn't it?" I said drily, aware that Eden was watching me, that glint of amusement still in his eyes. He knew I was annoyed and was wondering how I would deal with the situation. I promised him all sweetness and light. He had been fairly forthright in attributing base motives for my arrival at Lairigbrach. At least he wouldn't be able to put down unkindness to stepmothers or small dogs at my door.

"Where's Dad?"

"He took the children home. Er – Eden," again the sidelong glance "was kind enough to ask me in to wait for you and insisted that he would see me home."

"Perhaps Pearl would like to see the house," said Eden obligingly falling into her trap.

Apart from the drawing room, the other downstairs rooms were neat and tidy but exceedingly dull. Even Pearl blanched when Eden opened the door of Elliott's study across the hall. He hadn't been joking when he said Uncle Elliott's affairs were in a tangle. It looked as if a week's work lay ahead to put it to rights.

Eden closed the door hastily and Pearl trotted upstairs after him oh-ing and ah-ing at everything on the way, as if she were being shown around Buckingham Palace. TeeDee followed us, her female curiosity aroused aided by a certain reluctance to be parted from Eden, whose side (after her first rapturous greeting for me) she had leaned heavily against during the entire conversation. The fact that he received her favors with a certain amount of absent-minded unconcern did nothing to dash her hopes, or the nymphomaniac tendencies which kinkily preferred men to the males of her own varied species.

"This is my room," said Eden. It was something of a surprise. Characterless, an impersonal monastic cell, livened by a couple of bookshelves. Incredible, I thought, that he could have lived there fourteen years and left no trace of his own vivid personality.

He left us and I ushered Pearl into "Janet's Room." She came in cautiously, sniffing the air. In front of the canopied bed she hesitated. "Oo, what a spooky place. I wouldn't like to sleep here alone. Aren't you terrified, especially," she added in a stage whisper, "with that girl watching from the picture all the time." She giggled nervously. "And I don't like beds with curtains, anything might go on outside them and you wouldn't know until it was too late."

"Such as?"

Her eyes searched the corners. "Oh, I don't know. What would you do if you saw a ghost?"

"Probably scream the place down."

Pearl seemed comforted by this sensible approach to the problem and emerged after "spending a penny" charmed by my private bathroom, which outweighed the disadvantages of what she considered a "haunted bedroom."

"You are lucky, Lucy," she said as we went downstairs, "it's such a lovely house." In the hall, she looked upwards to the dark landing with a shiver. "But you know, I really do prefer a nice little modern house. I'd never be – comfortable – in an old house like this. I'd always be thinking of all the people who had lived and died in it and maybe were haunting it, just a little bit from time to time. I wouldn't be here at night on my own for a fortune. No street lights and that long dark drive with the bushes. And all those trees rattling up against the windows."

"One gets used to it, I suppose. There's probably a safe comfortable feeling, living where one's ancestors have lived for generations."

Pearl shrugged and looked at me doubtfully. "Who's *he*, anyway?" she asked, implying Eden. "Isn't he nice? Is he a relative?"

"Yes. From America."

"He doesn't sound like an American," she said in disappointed tones, her vision of Hollywood films, New York skyscrapers, oil millionaires and rich tourists all shattered. "But they do have such nice manners."

"He was only born there. He's lived in Scotland a long time."

"Does he manage the estate?"

"Not officially. He's a scientist."

"Scientist, eh. Nothing to do with atom bombs, I hope," she said anxiously.

"Nothing at all. He grows plants, I believe. Agriculture, you know."

"That's a relief." Scientists to Pearl remained a disreputable, disappointing breed, who invented boring things like bombs, moon rockets, computer societies, and sold state secrets to the Russians.

Eden strode into the hall, long, lean and graceful and Pearl watched him admiringly. I heard her sharp intake of breath and her voice raised one octave in acute politeness as she said, "All ready to go now. Sure I'm not taking you out of your way."

Eden bowed. "Not at all, a pleasure. I'll bring the car round."

Kissing me, she whispered, "Isn't he lovely?"

"I thought he might be your type."

"Silly," she said coyly. "I'm an old married woman."

"You're also a very dishy bird. And I think he's partial to blondes."

"Get away with you. He's more your age than mine."

"Thanks very much. But I have a feeling I'm not his type. He finds me rather dull, I fear."

"Don't be daft," she said, but without much conviction. "You know, he's not particularly handsome, but there's something about him. Has he got Spanish blood? Lots of the Americans do, I read somewhere."

I thought of the Conquistadores and the Plains Indians and said, "Probably. He's from the west."

"How romantic. Oh, there you are, Eden. This is kind."

"Not at all. I have to go into Aberdeen anyway. I'm picking up my girl after the theatre."

"Oh, really," said Pearl rolling her eyes heavenward in my direction in a look of mock tragedy.

Well done, Eden, I thought. He was being very crafty, giving Pearl the message that there isn't any romantic entanglement or indeed any reason for her to inspect Lairigbrach regularly, on the excuse that her stepdaughter's virtue might be in danger.

Holding TeeDee in my arms I watched them drive away and chuckled a little as I wondered what Pearl would say if she had known her charming American was also a genuine American Indian.

Ten minutes later, I was in the kitchen making coffee when Nurse Duncan came in. "Thought I smelt something good." She made a great fuss over TeeDee. "Hello, pet. Where did you come from?

"What a sweet little dog. Oh, I love poodles, don't you?" And TeeDee puffed out her small chest with pride and the one-tenth of her that was genuine poodle glowed with delighted flattery.

I explained the situation and Nurse Duncan said, "Oh, so that was your stepmother leaving with Eden. She's very young looking. Pretty too." And as if this set off an interesting chain-reaction, she added, "I saw you arrive earlier. With Dr Faro," and waited smiling, scenting a romance. "Such a splendid fellow," she added hopefully. "All the patients adore him. However, if he wants to succeed in general practice, he'll need a wife. Time he chose some nice girl."

She threw in an arch glance at that. All on the strength of one lift to Aberdeen and one movie together. It seems that for middle-aged women there's no place for single girls or single men in their schedules. They can't rest until they have the young paired off together, obediently trooping into the ark, two by two.

87

To my hasty query about Elliott, she replied, "He's sleeping a lot just now." I wondered when he would want to see me again.

"Well, he wanders a bit just now. It's to be expected towards the end. Talks a lot about Drew – " she coughed hastily, remembering I was Drew's widow. "We must just keep hoping, mustn't we?"

Her professionally bright nursing manner didn't fool me. Her tone suggested there was surprisingly little anyone could hope for.

"I wonder how long Miss Rosanna MacAeden will be staying with us?"

When I said I didn't know, she gave me a sly look. "I expect we shall see the fur and feathers fly between Miss Grantly and her. Understandable of course, since Miss Grantly has more right to Lairigbrach than anyone else, even the old gentleman himself. He inherited from his uncle who was *her* unacknowledged father, her mother, his housekeeper, was loyal and faithful to him for more than quarter of a century. And during that time, she remained obstinately Roman Catholic, refusing to divorce her husband whose name Alison bore. Shhh," she said warningly, "that's her car now. She'll know we've been talking about her. I'm off. See you later."

Alison greeted me cheerfully, disposed to be friendly. As both she and Eden had what Dickens had called "expectations," I wondered in their positions if I would have been so magnanimous to a last-minute usurper.

"Best thing you can do with this place, Lucinda is to sell out. Land on the North Deeside Road costs the earth these days. City's expanding in all directions. Skyline's a rash of great flats. Damned sensible, I call it. Nobody in their right mind wants a white elephant like Lairigbrach."

She asked about Elliott. "Sounds as if he's sinking fast. Nurse Duncan tells me he imagines Drew – er, well, all the departed MacAedens coming back. Gives me the creeps. I'm no hypocrite. Quite frankly, I'll be glad when the whole morbid business is over. This keeping him alive, when there's no hope of survival. Damned cruel. We do things to human beings these days in the name of medical science, we wouldn't do to our dogs."

She shivered. "Cold in here, isn't it. Come up to my room – it's cosy there – and have a nightcap. I have an electric kettle. No, can't sleep if I take coffee at night." Her room excellently lit by skylights, having once been an attic. It was large and untidy, like Alison herself. Inhabited by a wild selection of ghostly broken-down chairs and half-finished dresses on headless dummies. Books, magazines, erupted everywhere.

Paint-brushes sprouted in pots, potted plants cascaded wild leaves, boxes of chocolates, sweets, littered the mantelpiece.

Her taste in books was fascinating. Every conceivable religion. Mystic, pagan, the lot – and surely every word that had been written on ESP, the occult, spiritualism, astrology. On the walls voodoo masks vied with astrological charts. Yet strangely this cloak of mysticism seemed extraordinarily ill-made for such an unethereal, down-to-earth person as Alison Grantly.

Seeing my eyes wander to the walls, she made a gesture towards the charts, "Do you dabble?" When I said no, she sighed. "Pity. Felt quite certain the moment I first saw you downstairs that you were psychic." She sat back, considering me. "You have an aura, you know."

I smiled. "That's just Woolie's hair-lacquer, I'm afraid."

I regretted the flippancy when she gave me a hostile look, her sudden friendliness vanished. "I'm seldom ever wrong about people, you know."

"Sorry to disappoint you, but I've never seen a ghost in my life. Nor do I want to – "

She dismissed my sentiments with an impatient nod.

89

"There are other things than ghosts, my dear. Other ways in which the supernatural asserts itself."

I suppressed a yawn. The whole thing was a lot of old codswallop as far as I was concerned. It bored me, just as ghost stories, horror films, all bored me. The only odd thing I had ever experienced was that peculiar recurring dream about a red desert and the thunderbird, most probably the product of some childhood movie that had retreated into my subconscious mind.

She leaned over, took the empty tea cup from me, and still holding my hand turned it palm upward. "Fascinating, fascinating. It's all here. So well-defined too. A girl of infinite character, who knows what she wants. You will marry twice, I see. Drew's death is marked here. And Lairigbrach. There's something else. A great wilderness. Men on horses, danger, blood – something that happened long ago.

"How extraordinary. It doesn't seem to belong in your hand at all. It belongs – it belongs – as if there was another life before this one, another hand. I see a church. It's burning. There's a man, shot, dying – "

I snatched my hand away and Alison shook her head, blinked her eyes. She seemed to come back from a great distance. Her eyes were out of focus, she was breathing, heavily. She looked pale and exhausted.

"Why did you do that? What's the matter? What did I say? Did I see something? I did, didn't I?" she asked eagerly.

"Of course not. I'm sorry," I stood up. "I'm not meaning to be rude, but I just don't like having my hand read. Or my fortune told."

Leaning back in her chair, she watched me steadily. "Then I was right. I did see something. I was in trance, wasn't I?"

I shrugged. "How should I know?"

"Well, know this much. That it's dangerous to bring

90

someone back suddenly like that, when they're parted from their astral body."

I left her as swiftly as I could, with nothing to say. It really was too much. All this nonsense, this mumbo-jumbo.

On the way back to my bedroom, Nurse Duncan popped her head out of Elliott's room. "Yes, he's awake. Don't suppose he'll recognize you. But could you stay a minute, I have to phone for more pills."

I approached the bed cautiously, aware of the heavy silence, the ominous feeling that death was winning. It was stronger, closer now with life almost gone. His eyelids flickered.

"Uncle Elliott." They opened wide.

"Drew. Drew, my lad," he said in the strong voice I remembered. "I've been waiting."

"It's Lucinda," I said, without much hope of him understanding.

He chuckled. "I know it's Lucinda, but don't you see him behind you. Waiting by the door, beckoning to me. Drew – my boy."

Behind me footsteps. Almost terrified to turn my head, I sighed with relief as Nurse Duncan walked across to us. She shook her head.

"He doesn't recognize you. Poor old devil. Thinks everyone is Drew . . ."

Twice during the night I awakened with a voice calling for Drew. TeeDee beside me growled with fear. Suddenly sleep was gone and I thought about Alison. By what strange necromancy had she seen the red desert of my dream – my private hell?

I tried to rationalize the two apparently different sides of her character which did not compute. How she must have hated the MacAedens, as they fought their battles for the succession over polished civilized tables, the men smoking cigars, drinking brandy, instead of rushing down the heather-clad slopes of Kaimhill with claymore and dirk and wild plaids flying, screaming, "A MacAeden, A MacAeden," as they might have done four centuries earlier. While in the drawing-room the female of the species sat politely glowering over cups of coffee, planning the week's menus and deciding whether red was really a good choice for the curtains.

All this, instead of imitating their supposed ancestress Lady Macbeth and nipping smartly along corridors at dead of night, armed with deadlier weapons than soft drinks for an invalid uncle or hot water bottles for a chilly bed.

Viewed in retrospect, we were all nearer to Elliott's fanatical pretentions to Macbeth than even he dreamed. He was already conjuring up Drew from the dead, to creep along the dark corridors of Lairigbrach at the dead of night and like Banquo's ghost haunt our feastings on Ovaltine and digestive biscuits. One person at least despaired that "the old man had so much blood in him" and took such a long time in dying.

It was all growing uncomfortably close to Macbeth. Alison prophecying doom from my hand like a Witch of Endor. Elliott calling on Drew's ghost. It was a pity that Elliott was not present to witness the final scene and act of vengeance.

For this was the night that it all began. The Haunting of Lucinda MacAeden.

Chapter 9

I didn't sleep much that night. I got up early and took TeeDee for a walk. It was going to be a hot day, already insects were busily filling the morning with a microscopic orchestra; drumming, humming, whirring. The air was wine-clear and mist rising from the river trailed great white ribbons across the lawn.

The early morning sun gleamed golden on hills and river and pinewoods majestic, turning the landscape into one of those post-cards full of impassive stags and Highland cattle against impressive backgrounds in truly impossible colors.

The foreground was a stage set straight from "The Sleeping Beauty." On the steps I found I was imprisoned behind a gigantic web of gossamer which had been mysteriously but patiently spun during the night. It sparkled with dew drops and clung where it touched to my face, hands and arms. Leaving the house was like breaking out of some castle under a spell of enchantment. Occasionally TeeDee darted into the white ribbons of mist and vanished to reappear some distance away, a shadowy gray dog apparently walking effortlessly on cloud . . .

My destination was Macbeth's hunting-tower, but as it lacked doors or windows and only one wall, well-crumbled, remained, there was little evidence of long-departed glory. A melancholy sight for six o'clock on a summer's morning. It belonged to moonlit nights, with bats on wing and owl calls. Ruined towers are autumnal and best viewed at the height of their ghostly season. A

Sunday morning in high summer reduced the Gothic to a pile of old stones. It is not for them.

Later, when I returned I was astonished when Alison, bustling about the kitchen, announced there was to be a sherry party that morning after church. She said severely, "It's been a tradition in Lairigbrach for more than fifty years."

Later I learned that one or two ministers had raised teetotal objections, but the present incumbent, a man of enlightened views and a taste for argument, was delighted to warm both his hands and his backside in winter before the drawing room fire. In summer, he walked the lawns, oblingly expounding upon the more intricate parts of his sermon and with true Christian charity, broadmindedly smiled upon the section of what were geographically his "little flock," while pretending ignorance of the fact that they would never appear in his church for aught but "hatches, matches and despatches" (as he heartily referred to his parochial duties), and twice-yearly communion.

Attempts at sudden conversions or a too unsubtle display of religious propaganda were (like going home tiddly or worse falling into the shrubbery in a drunken stupor), the grossest forms of abuse of Lairigbrach's hospitality and both were severely frowned upon.

Without Elliott's presence as ring-master there was a tendency to anti-climax. An almost funereal atmosphere prevailed, with whispered conversations and anxious glances at the upstairs window. However, Alison took over as ring-mistress and played the part of lady of the manor to perfection to the large number of local landowners and university people who respected Elliott as historian as well as the laird of Lairigbrach.

Her gear for this occasion was somewhat startling. Her top half was faded *Carmen* straight from the cigarette factory. And from the waist down a thick, long, black skirt and stout black laced shoes, suggested one of the singing nuns erupting from the chorus in *The Sound of Music*. All, I suspected, had been specially imported with an eye to the imminent funeral, and was getting its debut today.

Much to my distress, Alison seized the occasion to introduce me as Drew's widow with a flourish of suitably mournful affection and soulful comments that "Drew had only gone beyond." She accompanied these remarks by raising her eyes and staring anxiously into the middle distance as if he had nipped behind a tree to attend to some gentlemanly need and would indeed be back with us in good time for a second glass of sherry.

Soon I was receiving whispered commiserations from dear old ladies who had "missed" me at the funeral, and from elderly worthy gentlemen, severe in countenance but sincere enough in manner. All suggested that Drew's fatal charm had irradiated even the stoutest Aberdonian hearts.

I heard the minister asking after Eden. "Haven't had our usual religious discussion," he said heartily. "A very well-informed young man."

A few of the old ladies tittered and exchanged glances, indicating that Eden made a nice fireside subject for discussion, doubtless his dubious ancestry and amatory pursuits came in for special attention.

I looked at the treetops. With wild clouds soft and white as fleece gathering along the Deeside Hills, as we humans walked on the bright lawns, from a bird's eye view we must have resembled a ragged clumsy assortment of dangerous beings, in our dull after-church Sunday plumage.

Suddenly Eden was there, strolling towards us. He looked detached and rather ill-tempered. Bored, bored, bored . . . Then a car swept down the drive and he brightened as a pretty blonde girl drew up alongside him.

This was Gillian, I learned later, daughter of one of the local bigwigs and according to Alison "filthy rich."

So that's why he doesn't need Lairigbrach, I remember thinking.

Eden leaned against the car, talked to her earnestly. He was obviously inviting her to stay. There was some argument and she shook her head, let in the clutch and drove off, leaving him scowling.

For a while he mingled with the guests, talking, smiling, a gravitational point for ladies of all ages. I, who had walked on the fringes of crowds unnoticed all my life, thought with a moment's envy how wonderful it must be to appear and have everyone surge towards you as if by the power of a magnet.

I sighed and Alison came over from answering the telephone in the house. "A reprieve, thank God. Rosanna's got a cold and has decided to come by the sleeper from London tonight. Let's all enjoy another day of freedom. Next Sunday she'll steal this show," she added ominously. "I hope she leaves all her tarty clothes in Dorset. They'd be most out of place here. Loves showing off her big fat legs. Thinks she's really something." She laughed viciously, rushing over to spread the news to Eden.

TeeDee spotted him, bounced out of my arms and away across the grass. Eden caught her deftly, brought her back. "Heard the glad tidings?" He looked frowning at the groups of dark figures. "Enjoy this sort of thing? I didn't think it would be quite you, somehow. Well, care to get away from it all? I have a picnic for two already packed and in the car."

I surprised myself by saying, "Yes, thank you, I'd love that," very eagerly in case he changed his mind. Especially when common sense told me that the picnic had been intended for the blonde girl in the car. But my main reason was anxiety to escape from another doleful day at Lairigbrach. Particularly from the shadows cast by a dying man who wasn't doing my nervous system any good by insisting that he saw Drew at regular intervals.

96

"Bring a swimsuit," said Eden as I ran into the house.

"What a good idea," said Nurse Duncan, busy at the kitchen sink. "You young folk can't be expected to sit around all day in this depressing atmosphere. Wish I was young again," she said with a sigh, watching Eden through the window.

"Come along," he shouted. "Stop gossiping, you two. Yes, yes, bring the dog." As I clambered in beside him, he grinned and blew a kiss to Nurse Duncan.

"Like the beach?"

"Oh, yes," I lied with a sinking heart. Was it only a week since depressed and full of forbodings of disaster (none of which had happened, of course, it's usually the disasters that don't forbode which overtake the unwary), I had taken the twins and Timmy to the seaside? I remembered that crowded beach, watching them shriek and splash as I huddled, sick at heart, against the promenade wall on the dry sand among the empty coke tins, orange peel and ice-cream wrappers. And scanning the crowds I had been on the look-out for the possible emergence of my Barbaric Stranger . . .

Now one Sunday later, I knew him, I was sitting at his side going off on a picnic to the beach . . .

"This isn't the way to the beach," I said accusingly, aware that we were going across country, heading north by a number of tree-decked, hilly sideroads.

"It is. To my beach," said Eden, giving me a mocking glance. "Do you mind? It's a secret place I discovered years ago."

"Sounds fun," I said and relaxed, thankful that we weren't going to be surrounded by screaming children and noisy transistors.

The hills retreated and the countryside flattened out into a patchwork of fields in greens and yellows. Sparse trees, leaning against the wind. Winding roads through sand-dunes. Someone had called this land of Buchan "the

97

cold shoulder of Scotland" and there couldn't have been a more apt description anywhere.

Then there was only faded waving grass. Down a sharp twisting lane Eden parked the car. As he switched off the engine the blue sky was full of the sound of larks singing, hundreds of them invisible above our heads but mad with summer joy. And all around us the smell of the sea.

Eden took out the picnic basket and tartan travelling rugs. "Right. It's quite a distance, roughish going. Can you carry one rug over your shoulder? Let's go. Through this gate and across the field here."

We could have been on a deserted planet where man had thrown down a communications system of telegraph wires, fences, and hurriedly departed. We walked, we trudged, through sand and there was no sign of other human life. Nothing. Only field, sand-dune, sky, sea-birds and larks unseen held sway. Then suddenly we seemed to walk off the edge of our strange world. Fields, empty but moving, behind us and far below, the sea on rock, the pulsating life of the ocean, rolling inwards as if it stretched out an enormous hand to gather us to its heart.

"Like it?," said Eden and before I could reply, "Careful from here on." And we slithered down a sandy path on sheer cliff-face. I followed him, groping for footholds, occasionally stumbling and grasping at the long grass, but he was sure-footed as a mountain goat. Carrying basket, rugs, TeeDee under one arm, he never stumbled once. Once he paused, warned me, "It's bad going. Take care. On a windy day it's suicide, you can be blown down to the beach, crash on to those rocks down there and you won't get up again . . ."

Miraculously, it seemed, we reached the pebbled shore all in one piece. There was a tiny stretch of sand not much bigger in area than the lawn we had left at Lairigbrach.

Behind us a great dark cave yawned into darkness. Big enough for a man to stand up in, to build a fire. There was evidence of fires made by Eden through the years.

And that was all. A tiny private world. The breeze that had harassed our walk down the cliff face had gone. This place was sheltered, enclosed, warm. The rocks jutting out to sea formed a lagoon with deep blue waters, remote from any suggestion of the cold North Sea, exotic as a South Sea island film set.

"Hungry?" asked Eden, opening the picnic basket. I said yes and he produced a roasted chicken, hard crusty rolls with garlic butter, fruit, and two bottles of wine. Two bottles. My eyes widened. With a capacity of about two glasses, I gathered he must have some very hard-drinking girl friends.

TeeDee galloped away to inspect the rocks and disappeared from sight. I called her. Nervous when she was out of sight, sure that another shoe box lurked to capture her, carry her out to sea, out of my life, for ever. I still shivered at the split-second rescue which Destiny had planned to land me with a dog of my own. "TeeDee, come and eat," I called.

"TeeDee, that's a hell of a name for a dog," said Eden in disgust, tipping a large measure of wine into my glass. "Why didn't you call her Growler, or Rover, or something doglike? What on earth does TeeDee mean?"

"Total Darkness."

"You're joking."

I stood up, scanned the horizon for her. Sighed with relief when a black woolly croquet hoop of hindquarters rose in the air, head and front paws hidden in the sand.

"Sit down. Relax," said Eden, sitting cross-legged on the rug and gnawing a piece of chicken. "She'll be all right, your Total Darkness."

I found I was thirsty, quaffed half-a-glass of wine at one gulp and was convulsed with merriment. From where I sat, all Eden needed was a wigwam at his back and a few feathers in his hair.

"Share the joke?" (No, I couldn't.) "Total Darkness. Now that's some name. How come you chose a corker like that when you bought a dog? Aren't there dog-naming books? Like the ones they have for babies?"

"I didn't buy her. I found her." And suddenly she rushed back, all covered in wet sand, but with the good manners of the poodle contribution of her ancestry waited on the very fringe of the rug, one paw upraised, head on side, all polite eagerness for chicken.

"You found her? How come?"

Softened by wine, suddenly I wanted to tell Eden, have him see I wasn't all harpy, sucking up to Elliott and trying to oust Alison and him from their rightful places in the pecking order at Lairigbrach.

It was just after Christmas, that depressing time when there are still decorations in the windows and streets, but inside the gift wrapping and the trees begin to look silly. People are fed up with parties and drink and the telly, the childrens' toys have all been broken or kicked to death, or their noise is driving their parents mad. That adorable puppy someone gave them is just a damned nuisance, yapping and making messes all over the kitchen floor.

On the day I found TeeDee, it was Fiona's aunt's birthday and by the time we had delivered her parcel, eaten shortbread and Christmas cake, it was too late to go anywhere but Nigg for the shells Fiona's little sister, abed with measles, had been promised to make animal figures.

And just a few hours earlier, somewhere in Aberdeen or its precincts, last week's Father Christmas had taken off his cheery beard and when the kids were out of the way, had gone down to the beach with a box and strict instructions to "drown the little b——. We'll tell the kids it ran away. They'll never miss it. They got bikes, a radio, wild west outfits. Games they haven't opened yet . . ."

Perhaps this genial ex-Santa lost courage or wasn't much hand at tying parcels, for the shoebox (Size 5, Ladies pink velvet slippers), didn't obligingly sink (with TeeDee frantic inside, clawing, crying), but instead floated on the tide and became wedged, waiting for death at high tide, in a hollow beside a rock pool.

Fiona said the seagulls were noisy. I said it sounded more like an animal. She agreed and as we walked over for a closer look, I was already green at the gills at the prospect of finding a dog with a broken back at the base of the cliffs. No hand at all with sick or wounded animals, fate usually conspired to bring me in for the death throes, in time to stand around and utter empty words of comfort and watch them die, helpless in my human fashion. All my life I've been haunted by the reproachful eyes of dogs or cats hit by cars, or dying fledglings or sick rabbits, never with even the strength of will to render the *coup de grace* and put them out of their misery.

There was nothing wedged in the rocks, Fiona warned. It was total darkness. But I knelt down, stretched an arm as far as it would go and was rewarded by a soggy shoebox which wobbled obligingly into my hands. A whimper inside, a soaked bundle of black wool almost unrecognizable as puppy until it moved. Shocked, shivering, but miraculously alive; gratefully but weakly wagging a forlorn stump of tail at us.

Tucking it inside my coat we fled back to the car. Where do we go from here? What about the Cat and Dog Home?

But as the scrap of wool felt warmth and huddled closer in my arms with a sigh of content, I couldn't do it. I couldn't abandon her again. Fiona's policeman father owned a guard-dog. That was out. I decided to face wrath at home with the hope that Dad and the children would stand up for me. I knew that neither stepmother Pearl nor her fat spoilt corgi Fitzie, would be delighted.

"And that's how she came to be called Total Darkness."

She had drifted to Eden's side during my story. I had seen his face darken with anger. Twice he swore. Now he said, "Come to think of it, Total Darkness couldn't be more appropriate." He lifted her in one hand and held her at eye level. "There's not much poodle in you, my girl, except for your coat. That long nose never belonged to a poodle and your mammy must have flirted with a spaniel by the look of your big, floppy feet." He put her down. "You may not be much poodle, but you're a hell of a lot of dog. Here's some chicken. Off you go."

We watched her as she ate, with tender approving glances, like parents of a sick child whose appetite needs encouragement. "Aren't you glad only her nose turned out to be Afghan Hound? Imagine if you'd taken home something that grew and grew like a Dog Mountain? Pearl would have been cross."

"That is a superb understatement."

He chuckled. "That Pearl. She's quite a dish."

"The competition has always been fairly keen," I remarked drily.

"What happened to your own mother?"

"She died."

"More wine?"

I took it. I had taken too much already, but I wasn't yet prepared to tell Eden (or anyone else) how my mother had died.

I had presumed from hints picked up here and there that she died at my birth. Neatly, tidily, like a heroine of a sad Victorian novel. It wasn't until a couple of years ago that Pearl, in a fury, put me right. In a moment of post-natal blues she had taken an overdose of sleeping pills. They found us together on the bed, me kicking happily, goo-ing by her side, she already asleep far beyond their waking.

There was an immediate feeling of self-disgust that a fat, happy, placid baby could have lain like a great slob and let

102

her mother die. I had seen pictures of her, beautiful but rather frail-looking. Then Pearl said I was one of those babies who never slept – and stopped suddenly. I knew then that I had driven a sick harassed woman to suicide to escape from me.

Guilt was born in me then. Guilt and the feeling that everything dreadful that had happened to me – Drew, the baby – even the Haunting of Lucinda MacAeden and the hint of madness – all were part of a giant scheme of expiation of my guilt at uncaringly letting my own mother die.

Chapter 10

"And what do you think of my secret beach?" asked Eden.

I shook off my doleful thoughts. "It's super."

"Good. Sometimes I feel a crying need to get back to the bare bones of the world, the earth and sky and sea. As it was in the beginning before the Almighty had leisure to add all the frivolous embroidery – like trees and rivers and people. Before God made Lairigbrach."

He smiled. "See that cave back there? Well, I've slept in it many times. Perhaps that satisfies a need too, seeing that my Pueblo ancestors were cavedwellers."

"What was it like – for you – before Elliott came?"

"The Navajo boarding school was bearable. I was one of the bright stars. The gifted part-Indian child. Their eyes widened. They talked about me in hushed tones as if they had discovered a freak – a horse that talked, or a fish that could walk. Meanwhile back on the Reservation – a lot had been happening. My people had forgiven my father for dying in a war that was the white Americans' war and no concern of his. But they had not forgiven my mother's death, because even as a war hero's widow, she had no pension. Nothing. Until too late, when she was already dying of tuberculosis, they rolled along in their great automobiles, with their Stetson hats and cigars and cameras."

He stopped, looked at me, running the sand through his fingers. "To us, They were the enemy, always. My people wanted a saviour, a leader and thought they had found one in me. Then along came the Boss – who was undoubtedly one of Them. Of course, he found countless Indians eager and willing to help him in his search when they saw the flash of mighty dollar bills and they remembered the whisky it could buy. In no time at all he could have had them queueing up to swear that Eisenhower himself was Chief Atala and Janet MacAeden's descendant."

"But wasn't MacAeden your father's surname. Isn't Eden just a corruption of it?"

He shook his head. "That was the convenient tag, the reservation and the boarding school put on me. Officially I was Navajo on my mother's side. Navajos have only secret names. They believe that to call a man by his real name is to steal his spirit. Mine was 'He Talks to the Ground'. How's that?" Eden smiled. "Worse than TeeDee, eh?

"The only relatives I remember were an old grandfather, Atala's son, Chief Ramez Atala, who had long since retreated with his peyote, his rituals, into the world as it was before the white man came. He used to beat the hide off me, if I used American words. Sometimes he would break out of the reservation, carry on a one-man war and have to be put in jail until his peyote 'visions' subsided. A great old man, he died when I was ten. His wife, my grandmother, would have sworn anything for whisky money and what she hopefully called 'a good time' from a rich white man.

"She made nice copy for the tourists sitting outside her hogan all dolled up in a tribal dress no Atalos or Navajo woman had ever worn. When she was young and not too fat, she did a good song and dance act around the small town music halls – "

"Wait. If this grandfather was Atala's son, then you must be Janet's descendant."

Eden frowned. "Wrong again, my child. This is the very nutshell Elliott has been trying to crack all these years.

What you dear innocent Christians don't realize is that we heathens are not monogamous. Polygamy is the order of the day. Atala had other wives and children – before he took off with Janet. He was quite old when he met her."

"Old? You said he was thirty."

"That's old where I came from, where the life expectancy was about twenty-five, until the white man gave us the drugs to kill the diseases *he* had given us. In Atala's day, men matured early. It was quite usual to be chief of a tribe, married and father of a family at seventeen. You had to work fast then to keep the race going, to keep warriors to fight for your rights. If you accept that Janet was Atala's third or fourth wife, then you get the problem. He probably had ten children, say four survived and provided sixteen grandchildren. It's quite possible by these simple mathematics, that there are thirty or forty great-grandchildren lurking about. I am only one of them. And which great-grandmother is mine?"

"It's certainly complicated. But you don't look – "

He grinned. "Come on. Out with it. I don't look like an Indian. Well, the Atalas were far from being as bronze say, as the Apaches or Cheyennes. In fact, their skins were almost white, which gave rise to the old Atlantis theory. They had escaped from the sinking continent of Atlantis and made their way, by means unspecified, to the Sierra Nevada and their secret valley."

He had taken off his shirt long ago. There was the thunderbird around his neck. I pointed to it now. "Has it some connection?"

"The undisputed talisman of the Atalos. Atala is wearing this – or a very good copy in the only painting of him." Eden squinted down at it. "A curiosity. It ought to be in a showcase in some damned museum. Do you know something? It isn't gold, it isn't copper. It isn't any mineral *known on this earth*. How's that for a science fiction plot? Are the Atalos the real Martians?"

106

"It's fascinating."

"Fascinating, maybe, but fairly destructive to an earnest scholar like Uncle Elliott in his laborious and costly research to prove that a certain Indian boy is not any old descendant of Atala, but in particular of Atala and Janet MacAeden." He indicated the thunderbird. "These are the accepted proofs among primitive peoples, especially on reservations where agents were often ignorant and illiterate as well as corrupt. And how do even honest agents keep efficient records of people who hate and distrust all white Americans and complicate the issue by having secret names? Yours isn't the only race to know color prejudice either. Whereas a lot of white Americans get a certain kick out of saying Grandma was part-Cherokee, the Navajos are very proud of their pure blood. Just as your Highland Clans are and as the Atalos once were. That bitter-sweet love affair between Atala and Janet almost wiped out a whole tribe.

"Anyway, if Elliott had proved I was the right one, I would have been undisputed heir to Lairigbrach. Otherwise it was willed to Drew – or his next-of-kin, Rosanna – until you came into the picture – "

I protested and he held up his hand. "Oh no, Lucy. You can keep Lairigbrach. All I ever wanted out of it was the money and even that isn't important any longer – "

"Have you no feelings for Elliott?" I asked, slightly shocked.

"Sure I have. But I'm not a sentimentalist. Especially about Lairigbrach. I don't want to belong to anyone or any *thing*. Mark my words, Lucy, the only quality left to value in this overcrowded hamstrung world is independence. The right to move like a free man.

"To me, Lairigbrach is just a pile of stones, an archaic tradition and I'd be happy and conscience-free to see hundreds of people living in skyscrapers where it stands. Naturally I'm sorry to disappoint the Boss, but I did warn him right at the beginning, that staying power wasn't my specialty. After all, I didn't ask to be brought to Scotland to be set up and bowed to as the heir to Lairigbrach. Until he found out that I was a phoney and blamed me for cheating him.

"If it comes to that, I already was someone, back in Arizona. Heir to the Sun-God, Chief Eden Atala waiting to lead his people to victory. I had been through the puberty ritual years before, and had emerged with my prophetic vision, my sacred dream. The singers had declared I was their true leader, a true descendant of the great Atala."

He sighed, hugging his knees and stared away beyond the bright cold North Sea. "I had a destiny, Lucy, and the Boss took me away from it and bought me like an old-fashioned slave in a Roman market-place. He paid for me with three hundred lousy dollars. Melodrama wasn't in it."

For a moment he was silent, watching the sand trickle through his fingers.

I said, "The slave turned into an excellent scientist according to Hamish. And a fine musician."

Avoiding my eyes, he answered, "Pop stuff."

"I've also heard you play in the symphony orchestra."

"So what? Maths and music often provide oddly congenial bedfellows." He smiled at me mockingly. "Don't fool yourself, sweetie. I'm just a lazy good-for-nothing Indian at heart."

"I don't believe it. Some of this – civilization, this middle-class British life you pretend to despise so much – must have brushed off on you through the years. You don't even sound like an American."

I had said the wrong thing. Eden sprang to his feet and drew himself to his full six feet. He looked down his nose at me in utter scorn. "I beg your pardon? You do, of course, mean a 'white' American. Seeing I have a language of

108

my own – I spoke only Navajo and Atalos until I came to Scotland, it's hardly surprising that I don't have an American accent." He laughed suddenly and pulled me to my feet beside him. "What on earth do you expect? Pidgin English?" He thumped his bare chest. "Me Atala – you Janet? That old routine or would you like a drawling westerner straight from a great epic. Ah, shut up, honey," he drawled, mocking me. He wagged a finger in my face and added seriously, "Don't start crusading. Have some more wine instead."

Bottle in hand, he smiled. "We're all doomed and me more than most. It's all the fault of progress. Bows and arrows to washing machines in three generations when it took the Western world nearly a thousand years. Have a heart – you can't expect wonders. Charming as we are and a boon to the tourist world and the glossy geographical magazines, we poor aboriginals have our limitations. We do lip service to many things to please our white brothers, but don't forget the inner ferment."

"I believe you're interested in religion, too."

Eden grinned. "Ah, yes, I see our jovial parson has been busy over the sherry. But did he tell you the answer to the vital question? Religious about what? I lost my old gods long ago, Lucy, when I was taught to see them as only painted masks. Whether they were the same as the Old Man Up There, I'm not prepared to argue. I'll never know, will I? My sacred puberty dream was probably hallucinations brought on by an empty belly."

He shivered, but not I thought with cold. "You know, I think what I need is a swim. Coming? No? Well, make free with the wine when I'm gone."

I watched him run down to the sea, thinking he had a very beautiful body and gorgeous legs in the briefest of shorts. I lay down on my rug, with TeeDee tucked into my side, and closed my eyes.

Too much wine, too much sun. I awoke to find Eden leaning over me, running a hand across my bare back.

"Relax, Carrot-Top. Nothing personal, only suntan lotion. The lady's not for burning. You'll be red as your hair tomorrow – only mad dogs and Englishwomen sleep out in the midday sun."

I kept my eyes tight closed and nodded vaguely, afraid of the feelings his hands brought, practical and business-like, clinically spreading lotion. The flicker of desire I had not known for years, the hunger for arms and lips and a strong body . . .

Fool that you are, it's the wine. Wine was always your downfall. First with Drew, a couple of glasses too many and see the disaster that it brought. I shouldn't drink. It made me amorous or sleepy . . .

"All right. You'll do." He stretched out on his rug and turned on the radio. Music filtered, gently, deliciously, through the afternoon sun. After the closeness of our conversation, it was oddly sensual, bringing awareness of the question unasked but understood between us. Or maybe all the closeness existed only in my eager imagination and he who had brought so many girls here before me, was just playing his game at his place. Perhaps he was even disappointed that I didn't respond.

Then suddenly, almost it seemed before it had begun, it was over. Four hours had incredibly passed. We were packed and climbing the steep cliff-face and I looked mournfully back at the little cove, now sunless, chilly, somehow lonely with the marks of our feet and the rugs, and TeeDee's pawmarks on the wet sand, already blowing away in the sudden wind.

We spoke little on the way to the car, needing all our breath to climb. The wine fumes had cleared from my head but there was something I had to say to Eden before Lairigbrach, and Rosanna, and Drew's shadow – and all my doubts – closed in on me again.

110

"It's been a lovely day." I hesitated. "I'm sorry, sorry we didn't meet in happier circumstances, that is," I added stiffly.

Eden laughed. "You sound exactly like a Jane Austen heroine. What's wrong with these circumstances, anyway. They seem all right to me." Swiftly he came round the car to my side. "Don't let it throw you, Lucy. My prospects, my expectations at Lairigbrach don't worry me one bit. They never have been part of my destiny, you know. So don't go all broody on my behalf."

He leaned over and cupped my chin in his hand. "There, there." His head bent down and he kissed my mouth and somewhere deep inside me there was a sudden twist. As if a glacier had left its moorings and started to move –

Then I wondered as my heart-beat settled to normal and he drove quickly, silently, whether he was regretting the kissing. Had it been only an impulse of kindness? In no time at all, I was back at my old game of torturing myself with doubts and self-examinings.

He didn't seem disposed to conversation as the miles slipped away behind us and when I threw in a remark about the weather or the scenery, he responded with an absent smile. All too soon, we were speeding back along the North Deeside Road, down into the hump and hollow of walled houses. The trees threw great zebra-striped shadows across the leafy road, packed with cars returning from Deeside and Sunday afternoon picnics. I was heartily glad of Eden's lonely beach, already it had taken on a dream-like quality of unreality. Some day it was a memory I would take out and remember and treasure.

We slid down the shadowy drive and there was Lairig-brach, its lawns empty, the house dark on this side against the sun, gloomy, uninviting. At the steps, Eden switched off the engine and put his arm along the back of my seat. "Well, Lucy. Home again."

I smiled bleakly hoping he was going to kiss me again.

111

Perhaps the message was received and understood for despite the windows of the house gazing down at us (and at least one of them containing Nurse Duncan), he leaned over and his lips brushed my cheek.

And suddenly deep inside me, the glacier moved again. Desire awakened, long after the wine fumes had departed. In a dream I followed him out of the car, holding his hand like a child. He threw his jacket over his shoulder and we walked up the steps and into Lairigbrach. As he opened the door, he looked down at me and smiled. He understood . . .

The sound of a horn behind us, another car on the drive.

"Gillian," he said and looked at his watch. "Is it that late? Almost forget our date." He grinned apologetically. "I'll just unpack the car."

I held out my hand for the keys. "Let me do it for you."

"Sure you don't mind?"

"Sure." I could at least still be a gracious loser.

I watched him run down the steps to the girl with her lovely blonde hair and her elegant white sports car. He leaned over and kissed her on the lips. There was nothing in that kiss to remind me of why I should blush at the brotherly way he touched my cheek moments ago.

Angrily I closed the door, hating Gillian's delighted laugh. Rich too, was she? It seemed that Eden had done his sums very well and come up with the perfect answer to his problem.

I unpacked the hamper, washed the dishes, disposed of the sand. Returning the rugs to a shelf in the cloakroom cupboard, I dislodged a vividly checked raincoat from its hanger away at the back of the rail. It was oddly familiar. I knew why as I picked it up and read the label.

Drew, naturally distrustful of everyone when he was on tour, always carefully labeled his possessions. It must have been left here on one of his infrequent visits. With a feeling of nausea, as if his skin had brushed mine, I replaced it.

Suddenly I wanted to talk to Fiona. I needed a shoulder to cry on, but when I dialed the number, her mother told me she was visiting Dick's married sister in Edinburgh for a few days. But what about the office, I asked?

Surely I had heard? Our boss decided to close down as it was hardly worth paying salaries with the business now involved. Fiona had tried to contact me. No doubt she would be in touch when she got home. Of course, with her wedding only weeks away, she wasn't on the look-out for another job. And how was I?

I was still awake when Eden returned that night. Janet's eyes had been smiling from the portrait and set me thinking about the past. How this house had been modern when she left for California, never to return. How the whole of Aberdeen must have looked then – newer, sharper, brighter. The suburbs now so magnificently Victorian, the great houses in Queen's Road and Rubislaw Den, the mansions of the newly-rich from fish and granite.

There would be more trees in the streets, more farms on the outskirts and Lairigbrach must have appeared quite isolated, in the very heart of the countryside where now buses and cars roared past the lodge gates, carrying commuters twice daily between Aberdeen and Culter, Banchory, Aboyne . . . The railway line on the southern fringe of the grounds was obsolete, overgrown, dead. A hundred years ago. Queen Victoria in her widow's weeds was still trundling up and down to Ballater in the Royal Train, to Balmoral Castle and assignations with John Brown. Bring her back and she would hardly recognize the Aberdeen skyline, that stern face would not be amused.

In another century Lairigbrach itself would be gone, this whole area a housing-estate with all traces of house and grounds vanished, the mad MacAedens, Janet's strange story, Elliott's proud claims to his family glory, all forgotten. Macbeth? Who was he? Oh, yes, only a character from Shakespeare . . .

At last I heard Eden come back. I rushed to the dressing-table, combed my hair, quickly sprayed on perfume, hoping he would bring a cup of coffee, as he did my first night in Lairigbrach.

But not tonight. I heard his light footsteps pass my door, his own door close. Angrily I got into bed and put out the light. Later I dreamed that Drew came in and stood by the bed, looking down at me, smiling, wearing the checked raincoat. The dream wasn't surprising. What was surprising this time was that I felt so little fear.

Chapter 11

The first round at Lairigbrach was definitely Rosanna's. By one of those curious coincidences Alison and Eden, who were to be her reception committee, both overslept. The first notice of her arrival was the taxi arriving and Nurse Duncan opening the door.

As three of us scrambled downstairs we did not present an inspiring picture for an elderly woman who was recovering from a severe cold and whose arthritis was particularly troublesome that day. These disasters she managed to convey to us within the first two minutes. She also added that the weather was so cold in Aberdeen, compared with Dorset, in reproachful tones, as if we were personally responsible for the climate.

She was not disposed to be friendly. Nurse Duncan saved the situation by rushing into the drawing room with a tray. "I've put on the electric fire, you'll be warm in no time. And here's a nice pot of hot tea and some toast. There now."

Rosanna received this kindness without comment as she also received Alison's profuse apologies and said acidly, "I suppose I'm not too late and that my cousin is still alive. It seems the way people can sleep in this house, one could die without being noticed."

I followed them into the drawing-room and squeezed Nurse Duncan's arm. "Bless you for that."

She winked. "Old battle-axe by the look of her. Thank heaven she's not my responsibility."

Pouring out tea, I decided that the MacAeden women had a monopoly on bizarre fashions. Rosanna was no exception. I suppose connections with pantomime in her prime had made me expect a rather well-developed over-blown blonde with a complexion like a wizened peach.

The blonde hair was there, vital and so luxurious that "wig" was the immediate suspicion. Later Alison shook her head, and said, "No, she always had marvelous hair. The best thing about her, I believe." Rosanna was tall for a woman with all those curves coveted by an earlier generation now corseted into rather solid-looking flesh.

Her make-up was heavy and dated. The husky voice a parody of the sexy image she had once enjoyed. She looked to my shocked eyes, like a rather aged tart – hardly the impression we had been given of a dusty Miss Haversham, eccentric and pining for a love long-lost. This Rosanna looked as if she might give nails lessons in hardness and durability. Under the gloss, I imagined a shrewd woman, calculating as any man, with little true softness or femininity.

When she removed her glasses to search in her handbag, I stepped back in horror as I had done with Elliott, for I looked into eyes despite the make-up, unmistakeably familiar. The MacAeden family looks were all variations on a single theme. Drew at its handsomest. Elliott at the seventh age. Rosanna and Alison had come off worst in a family which produced a uniform set of features for both males and females. What was handsome in the men was translated into big faces, heavy-featured, with large hands and feet in the women.

The only one who did not look at all like a MacAeden was Eden. His features provided by some ancient forgotten civilization, especially if the Atlantis legend were true.

Whatever Rosanna's reasons for coming to Lairigbrach, devotion to the family was neither immediate nor evident. She informed us that she would wait and visit her cousin when he was a little more recovered, at which we all exchanged glances. She stood up, said she had a sore throat, was cold and tired and asked for directions to her room.

We all trooped into the hall after her and Eden said, "I'll just take your cases and lead the way."

She looked up the huge flight of stairs with a heavy sigh. "Isn't there a room available on this floor? I have arthritis, you know, and I find it extremely difficult to climb stairs."

"I'm sorry," said Eden, "I didn't know that." So he was responsible for the hospitality at Lairigbrach, the lit fires, the flowers, the hot water.

"What about Elliott's study? As I remember it is across the hall there."

"See for yourself," said Eden, opening the door on a cascade of books and papers. "It will take a week to make it habitable. Besides the loo is upstairs."

"The loo?" she asked with raised eyebrows.

"There's just an outside one downstairs. Behind the scullery."

"My dear young man, I presume you mean the toilet."

Eden shrugged. "Call it what you will." He looked tired, impatient. "I prepared an upstairs bedroom where I'm sure you'll be very comfortable."

"I want one with a private bathroom, like the room I had on my last visit here," she said petulantly.

"Well, seeing it's just for a few days, the guest room facing south across the Dee is very pleasant," said Eden gently.

"What do you mean – just for a few days?" she said slowly.

At that, Alison and I exchanged despairing glances.

"God in heaven," murmured Alison in my ear, "surely she's not intending to stay for long."

"Hmm," said Rosanna, "my plans aren't made yet. And

117

who are you, anyway, young man. Are you an employee of my cousin's?"

I cringed at her tactlessness and remembered my own at first meeting with Eden. What must we sound like?

He looked at her levelly. "I live here. I'm Eden Atala – a kind of cousin."

"I did introduce you," said Alison reproachfully.

"Oh, indeed. My hearing isn't all that good, especially when I am cold." She took up her stick and leaned on it. "Eden Atala, eh? You look as if you've got a touch of the tar-brush to me."

I think both Alison and I must have gasped audibly at that, for she looked at us, her lips curling in a pleased smile, like a child delighted at her own outrageous behavior.

"I don't think you need lose any sleep over that, Miss MacAeden," came Eden's cool voice. "I'm not intending to be a permanent resident at Lairigbrach."

"I'm pleased to hear that," said Rosanna and turned her back on him, looking at Alison and me, grinning as if she had said something very clever. "Give me a hand upstairs, Alison, you're a sturdy-looking female. Your boy here," she nodded in Eden's direction, "can carry my luggage."

I followed them, as slowly, gasping, she made her way up step by painful step. I was deciding if she was in agony a lot of impatience must be forgiven her, but when we reached the landing it was my turn for the inquisition. She thrust out a large surprisingly strong hand and grasped my arm.

Peering into my face with narrowed eyes, she said, "And what about this one? Where does she sleep? Yes, you, Lucinda. You look pretty enough to have tricked my Drew into marriage. I asked where do you sleep?" Then she turned and looked insolently, meaningfully at Eden. "Perhaps in the servants' quarters? Or would that be an indiscreet question?"

Eden's lips tightened. "Lucinda has the room across

118

from the master bedroom. Elliott wished to have her near him in his last days."

"Came in nice time for the pickings, didn't you, my dear." She turned her back on me. "I think her room will do nicely for me. She can sleep around elsewhere, with the hired help. Ah yes," she threw open the door of my bedroom, "this is what we used to call Janet's Room. I remember it well. Best room in the house – "

Eden stepped in front barring her way. "I think you perhaps are a little deaf this morning. You didn't hear me correctly. This room is now Lucinda's, at Elliott's wish."

Rosanna shrugged, momentarily defeated by Eden's icy manner. She took Alison's arm. "Give me a hand to unpack. Paint, don't you. That landscape one of yours? Good, good." She peered at it. "Not bad at all."

Eden stepped aside and taking advantage of his move, she stepped into my bedroom. "The portrait room."

Janet looked at us smiling, welcoming, her head inclined in greeting.

Rosanna stared at the portrait, then at Eden. "So your grandfather was the child she got after Atala raped her." She laughed. "And how did my fool of a cousin ever hope to prove that you're a MacAeden. All right, all right. You two can go about your business. Alison here will show me the rest of the house."

We watched them go, Alison turning occasionally to make writhing, protesting faces at us. "So she knew all the time who you were," I said to Eden. "What a hateful old woman."

As we went downstairs, Eden said, "I think she's laying it on a bit thick. You know, playing her big scene. She realizes that being an eccentric is expected of her, so she's giving her best performance. At least I'd rather have her like that, know where I stand, than have her hypocritically playing all sweetness and light." He smiled. "Now's your chance to see the family drama in action, as the two ladies fight it out.

"Alison had hinted through the years that she could have been mistress of Lairigbrach any time she liked. She could have married her half-cousin Elliott had she not been dedicated to her career. And on the other side, we have the ex-fiancee, somewhat transient and unofficial, Rosanna.

"There's a strong streak of the theater in the Family."

"Which accounts for the guitar and the violin-playing."

"One of nature's small coincidences," said Eden. "The MacAedens see themselves as much bigger game, playing loftier roles . . . like Macbeth."

"That's a far cry from Rosanna's role as principal boy in pantomime, surely. Why didn't Elliott marry?"

"He's shy with women and a little afraid of them. He can't abide children either. So when he discovered Drew he thought he had found the easy way out. Drew would found a new dynasty of MacAedens for him."

Alison came into the kitchen, red-faced and mutinous. "Old bitch, she needn't think for one moment she's going to boss me about."

"There, there," said Eden soothingly. "In a few days we'll probably all be eating out of her hand. Allowances must be made for an elderly spoilt woman and a very untimely arrival – "

"Allowances, be damned," said Alison, as Eden Atala, scientist, gathered briefcase and books and set off to the research laboratory. There he did mysterious things with plants hoping for a break-through by which a process would emerge of growing crops successfully in any conditions and turning poor starved soil – like the area in Arizona where he had lived as a boy – into a rich fertile land.

But Eden was right about Alison and Rosanna. In a couple of days Alison was saying contritely, "Rosanna has

120

decided to take up residence in her bedroom. These stairs are really much too difficult for her."

Then we learned the real reason for the sudden friendship. They were soulmates. "Rosanna is a believer. She's deeply psychic," whispered Alison in wide-eyed awe. "She has had some truly remarkable experiences."

Having a fellow-psychic around impressed Alison enormously. From rebellion and instant dislike, she moved to absolute servitude in one bound. When she was present in Lairigbrach, there were no more complaints about it being her turn to carry loaded trays upstairs to Rosanna. Passing her on the stairs one day, I thought that for a semi-invalid and a sedentary woman, Rosanna had a truly formidable appetite.

Although her room was near Elliott's, she rarely visited him, content with reports on his condition. After the first time she said, "Not again in a hurry, I can tell you. He scares the wits out of me. How horribly he's changed and worse, he thought I was Drew." She shook her head. "I don't like this sort of thing, this 'calling on his soul within the house'. One shouldn't conjure up the dead. It can be very dangerous." For once I agreed with Rosanna.

Now that running the domestic side of Lairigbrach was my official duty, I set to work planning meals, baking, cooking and in any spare moments I wielded a vacuum cleaner and duster, or set about ordering the chaos in Elliott's study. For a most persnickety man, he had an alarmingly haphazard approach to business, his filing system a huge drawer in his desk, where all letters and their replies had been impatiently thrust.

Upstairs poor Elliott lingered in his twilight world and Hamish looked in with such frequency that Eden remarked teasingly, "It's really an excuse to see you. We must have a foursome one evening. Hamish and you, Gillian and me," he added cheerfully and my heart sank just a very little. But I wasn't sure of the reason – not then.

121

From Hamish over many cups of coffee, I learned some interesting things about the family. After Janet's departure, the nephew who eventually inherited, died insane, having chased his unfaithful wife through the grounds on horseback and trampled her to death deliberately.

"Suicides and insanities were frequent and until Elliott inherited they were an ungodly lot. Some very nasty traits, far more appalling than the usual lechery and lust. Sadism for one thing . . ."

I tried not to think of Drew. I wanted to make an emotionless, conscientious success of running Lairigbrach, without any personal involvement.

The days were passing busily and well. I could have been happy except that despite my exhaustion, I was sleeping badly.

Drew began to haunt me. It was so ridiculous that I couldn't bring myself to tell anyone, especially Alison and Rosanna, who would make such a psychic feast of it. Right at the beginning Lairigbrach had brought dreams of Drew, but this was worse. I knew I was awake, aware, hearing his footsteps, his voice calling "Lucy, Lucy . . ." Once the door handle turned.

Then came the night when, sleepless, I sat on the window-seat. A man walked towards the house over the lawn and into the moonlight. He looked up, saw me, smiled and touched his face in a grave familiar salute.

Drew.

I ran to the door, dragged at the knob. But it wouldn't open. I was locked in. I listened. Up the stairs, along the corridor the light sound of footsteps.

"By the pricking of my thumbs, something wicked this way comes . . ."

Nearer, nearer. And I was trapped . . . trapped . . .

The dream would continue as it always did. As if

by magic the locked door would open. Drew would be standing there, smiling.

A gentle tap on wood. A voice: "Lucy, Lucy . . ."

And without any help from me, as if by its own volition, slowly, the locked door opened . . .

Chapter 12

Eden caught me as I fell forward in a dead faint. When I came round, I was thrust back against the pillows while he forced brandy down my throat, cursing me as I resisted. "Take it easy. Having a nice sleepwalk, were you?"

But all I saw was a dark shadow. A dark shadow that was somehow Drew. I fought him off. The glass spilt. I wouldn't drink. I remembered too well, Drew with his abominable drug experiments, to make me quiescent, ready to play his games . . . and Tony's games too. I was back again in nightmare. I heard myself moaning, "I can't escape. I can't escape."

"Sure you can. Any time you like. You're raving. Drink this water, then, there's a good girl." The hand on my forehead was cool and gentle. "Nobody's going to hurt you. I'll look after you and keep the bogeymen at bay."

And Drew's hair had changed, darkened. I got my eyes into focus and he had turned into a young Heathcliff, ugly yet wholesome, brooding on the edge of my bed, chafing my hands.

I looked towards the window. Somewhere below in the haunted garden an owl cried and a night bird's lonely cry echoed shrilly across the sky and drifted away on the last of the moonlight.

"Eden," I said clutching his hand.

"Hello, Lucy. What happened to you? I heard you crying as I came past the door and then you went off in a dead faint."

"Drew. I saw Drew in the garden. Just before you came in."

Eden's eyes followed mine to the window. "Drew? You *were* dreaming then."

"No, not this time. I saw him walk towards the house. Across the lawn. He looked up, saw me and smiled. And don't tell me I was mistaken. I know it was him."

"All right, all right." He patted my hands for a moment, like someone soothing a frightened child. "Lucy, you *were* mistaken – yes, you were. That was me out there on the lawn," he said with a worried frown. "I couldn't sleep and I went for a walk, I was enjoying the moonlight. When I came back I saw you at the window and waved. Then I came upstairs and heard you cry out."

"But – "

"But me no buts, girl. It was me. I'm sorry, you must have been sleepwalking. Somehow you saw me and imagined I was Drew."

I leaned against the pillows. So it had all been illusion, hallucination. All those precious minutes kaleidoscoped into one awful second of – what? And deep inside a soft voice suggested: Madness?

I looked at Eden. Could moonlight have transformed him into a fair young man with a jaunty walk I recognized through a thousand nightmares, that mocking grave salute? What reason could Eden have for lying to me? For comfort, reassurance? Or was there something else, something that nagged, a half-thought still, a certainty that there was some deadly game afoot and I was unknowingly involved.

Was it a plot? Were all three of them – Eden, Alison and Rosanna in it against me? Did they cast aside their masks when I wasn't there and relax until next time I was on stage – to be tortured, tormented and frightened out of Lairigbrach, so they could use it for their own ends.

The alternative was diabolical. That I was returning to

the state I had been in when the baby died, fluttering uneasily, balanced on the very fringe of madness itself.

"Moonlight plays tricks with appearances," said Eden.

I shook my head. "There have been other times. I've heard him in the hall, outside my door. He tapped on it, called my name. I thought I dreamed, but now I'm not sure any more. I'm not sure of anything." Eden smiled tolerantly and I clutched his arm. "It's true, I tell you, it's true."

He smiled. "It's full moon and all this hovering on the brink of death. This talk about spirits is putting a jinx on the house. Do you know that Rosanna and Alison have an ouija board working overtime along the passage? They're getting plenty of mileage out of that bit of black magic."

I looked at Eden uneasily. "Perhaps they're conjuring up what is best left dead. Rosanna said something like that to me the other day. About Elliott calling for Drew, 'calling upon his soul within the house,' she called it."

"That's the 'Willow Cabin' scene from *Twelfth Night* and nothing to do with spooks. Rosanna must have an overdose of Shakespearean quotations."

But I wasn't listening to him, remembering Drew taken in death, so suddenly. Hating me, hating all of us, for going on living when life for him was no more. Taken away before he committed half the mischief, the disasters his craven soul thrived on. It was astonishingly easy to believe in Drew as just the kind of evil presence ghosts were made of . . .

I listened to Eden with his consoling jargon, his scientific explanations and watched him with some distaste. Why had he to be so thick about it? Why couldn't he see how deadly it was? Why couldn't he realize I was in danger.

"You make it sound as if I'm crazy," I said.

"Don't you think it's crazy to suggest Drew is haunting *you*. He was your husband. Why should he want to torment you from the grave?"

"That's an easy one to answer." I paused. "Because I didn't love him."

Eden looked at me. "I wondered about that. You turned positively green about the gills when the family eulogized over him."

"I loathed him."

"Good for you. So you found him out." And Eden smiled, a new light in his eyes. "'O, what may man within him hide, Though angel on the outward side!' Shakespeare, my dear, not our family favorite Macbeth this time, but another deep-dyed villain. And what did Drew do to you? It must have been considerable to turn love into hate after a few months of marriage."

"I don't want to talk about it. I can't tell you."

"Lucy," Eden took my arms, turned me to face him. "Don't you understand it's all this mix-up in your subconscious that's causing the trouble. If you want to sleep without nightmare, then you've got to tell someone. I'm cheaper, easier and less trouble than the psychiatrist's couch. Besides I'm on your side. I have a built-in sympathy for people who weren't Drew-worshippers. Even as a boy he was a ghoul, not just mischievous, but utterly corrupt."

"I can't talk about it. I can't."

"Please yourself. I'm only trying to help you. Lucy, if you go on suppressing all this, you'll end up with a breakdown."

"I've had one already."

"That's no guarantee you won't have another." He looked at me steadily. "To start off with, I think you ought to pack your bags and go right home to Pearl and your Dad. Now."

"I can't. I must find another job first, be independent. I hate living with them – there isn't room for one thing – "

"What the hell, Lucy? You can sleep on the sofa."

"I can't. Pearl doesn't want me there. I've always been

127

in the way. She adores Dad and thinks every time he looks at me he's remembering my mother."

"Your father is an attractive man. He married again. So what? Your own mother died, when you were a baby?"

"Oh, yes. She committed suicide because of me. When I was months old, because I wouldn't let her sleep."

Eden wasn't shocked. He merely shrugged. "I wouldn't make too much of that. A lot of mothers get post-natal blues. You can't blame their babies for that." He took me by the shoulders. "Snap out of it, Lucy. The past can never be changed, but the present can. And carrying a load of self-inflicted guilt is the quickest way to a nervous breakdown."

"You don't understand."

He sighed. "Well, I am trying hard."

"I promised Elliott I would stay at Lairigbrach."

"The Boss is long past caring, or knowing, whether you're still here. Alison and I managed before without help – "

"I promised. As soon as I'm released from that promise, I'll find another job, take a place of my own. Meanwhile, I'm *not* going home."

"All right, you're not going home." He paused. "If things get, well, tough here have you friends to go to?"

"I am not going to sponge off my friends."

"You are the most stubborn girl I know." He looked at me silently, frowning. Then he said, "You can move in with me. You can always come and live with me."

"What exactly does that mean?"

He smiled. "Not quite what you're so transparently thinking. I'm not going to set you up in a love nest." He laughed and his eyes raked over me rather approvingly, so that I drew the sheets closer round my neck. "Although I must admit, it doesn't seem such a bad idea."

"Oh, really," I said trying to sound discouraging.

"I have a flat in town."

"I thought you lived here at Lairigbrach."

"Well, I do – officially." And he had the grace to look somewhat uncomfortable. "The Boss doesn't know about it. I just prefer to have something that is completely my own. A place where I can take my friends. Damn your knowing look, Lucy – and don't grin like that at me. Yes, I do take girls there occasionally, but that isn't its prime purpose.

"I had to have a place where I could be myself, like my beach, without the claustrophobic atmosphere that pervades Lairigbrach. My place is a comfortable two rooms, small, warm, and I can get drunk, or play the guitar, or have an all-night party when the mood takes me. It's a refuge from the world, my refuge.

"I'm a grown man, in a few years I'll be thirty. And I've been a man a long time. Since I was twelve, the punishment for belonging to a different race where men mature earlier. Only children live with parents, or devoted relatives. Men and women need lives of their own. Anyway, if you're desperate – welcome to the flat with minute kitchen and shared bath – "

"Who do I share the bath with?"

He smiled. "You can have the bedroom, there's a divan in the other room." I looked at him sitting on my bed, Genghis Khan with a red scarf around his neck, his black hair, the strange dark eyes and too-big mouth. ("Too full of teeth" my friend Fiona said). It wasn't a handsome face, but a vital, oddly attractive one. A face I felt I could trust.

"Why are you doing all this for me, when all I'm doing is taking Lairigbrach away from you?"

"Don't talk like an idiot. All you're taking is a millstone away from me. Heavens, girl – I thought we'd settled *that* one. Why am I doing all this for you?" he said slowly. "I don't really know – I keep my bouts of self-analysis in such matters down to a minimum. Pretend, if it worries you, that I share your deep-rooted passion for little lost dogs and lame ducks – and you seem admirably qualified to join them." Suddenly he smiled, the slow enchanting smile. "Perhaps it's just because you're a pretty girl in distress appealing to my chivalric instincts. All men like to see themselves as Don Quixote."

"And if I came – what do you get in return?"

"What do you mean? What do I get in return?" he asked cautiously.

"Look, Eden, I know enough about men to know when I'm being – to quote our American friends – propositioned."

"Propositioned, be damned. You only know about scum like Drew. For heaven's sake, Lucy, don't take refuge in femininity with me. What do you want me to do? Offer a humane refuge in one breath, and splendidly propose on one knee in the next.

"All right, so I might sleep with you if you're encouraging, but don't try to lure me into the marriage game. I've known plenty of women in my time but I've never met one who was important enough for me to want to spend the rest of my life with – till death do us part.

"You can blame your civilization for that too – I probably haven't got the tribal addiction to polygamy out of my system yet."

Suddenly chilly, he stood up. "Well, Lucy, think over what I've said. Believe that I have your interests at heart and stop trying to read between the lines, to find out the hidden meaning, like most women do. Don't try to read what isn't written yet, not even in the stars. Shall we leave it that we like each other, we're *sympatique* and let's not make this the grand passion of the century."

I followed him to the door. "Eden, please. I do appreciate your kindness. I'm sorry I was rude about it. Forgive me." And standing on tiptoe I kissed his cheek.

"Good grief, girl," he growled, "I want better than

130

that." And taking me in his arms, he kissed me. No man, not even Drew on the small occasions of love between us, had ever made me feel so complete, so fulfilled as Eden did in that one kiss. I was loved, protected, cherished, adored. It was every love song, every line of Shakespeare – and to him it didn't mean a thing.

Yet I know if he had asked me then to stay, I would have said yes, and I knew too that I could never share that flat with him "in cold blood." All too soon, it seemed, he released me and said, "Go to bed, Lucy, you deserve all you get – kissing men in nothing but your nightie."

He laughed, patted my cheek and was gone, while I lay sleepless until dawn.

Alison's exhibition opened the following evening in a small private art gallery off Albyn Place. It was to be celebrated with a sherry party for the press and invited guests.

"Come early," Alison told me at breakfast, "before the crowd arrives. I'm always so nervous, I need moral support."

"And some physical support with the paintings, too, as I remember," said Eden. "I'll come straight from the lab and take you out for a meal, Alison, so that all the sherry won't go to your head."

"I've persuaded Rosanna to come along. It'll be a change, do her a world of good. After all, she is on holiday," said Alison rather apologetic about her concern. "She'll come in with me, wants to have her hair done and a look at the shops now that she's feeling better."

With no evening meal on schedule, I looked in to see Nurse Duncan. "Yes, do that. Have a day off. I don't know when you'll get another," she said, nodding towards the tiny shrunken figure in the bed.

Poor Elliott. If one drops dead in the street, friends and loved ones are shocked, stricken, but a long lingering death loses all nobility and drama, while relatives and friends await the inevitable end in a succession of weary anti-climaxes.

His eyelids opened as I approached. "Drew, my boy. Is it you?"

Nurse Duncan at my side shivered, "See what I mean – the poor old devil. Can't be long now."

I carried TeeDee's basket down to the kitchen and went along the drive feeling like a servant with the day off. At the bus stop a soft mist turned into drizzle and when I reached the house in John Knox Avenue, it seemed to have shrunk since my last visit, diminished in size by the rain.

Timmy and a particularly noisy friend came inside to play, stumbling over our feet with their toys and making coherent conversation impossible. Pearl used to chaos, watched the tennis on television, tried to make herself heard above the din and imperturbably knitted an Aran sweater for Dad. The twins arrived back from the zoo, rather damp and in shrewish moods. They were growing up and regarded me with silent aloof suspicion perhaps in sympathy with their mother's resentment of me. Suddenly I felt a hundred years old.

I threw myself into Dad's arms when he arrived. Over the meal the talk was all Lairigbrach. I longed to speak to Dad privately, confide in him my fears. I soon gave up. The house was like St Nicholas Street during the summer sales, and I left with a sigh of relief at seven.

In a few days I too had changed. After the peace and serenity of my days at Lairigbrach, where only the nights were haunted, the idea of returning home to John Knox Avenue appalled me.

At the Art Gallery, Alison and some of her students were hectically making last minute preparations while Rosanna watched implacably from the double settee, strategically situated in the center of the room. Sipping sherry, she was a bizarre stout figure with bright blonde curls, heavy make-up and tinted glasses. At least she was disposed to be friendly.

"This is such an occasion and I get so few these days," she said in her husky voice, departing on the sturdy arm of a bearded student who invited her to look at the other exhibitions showing in the gallery. She gave me an arch look, holding his arm with one large hand, fingernails painted bright red (presumably also for the occasion) looking somehow predatory, sharp as talons. I watched them walk away, oddly repulsed by this travesty of an overweight 'thirties film star.

Alison's landscapes and the entire room were dominated by a portrait of Eden ("Not for sale" said the catalogue.) Eden, as he might have been before civilization channeled him into scientist, amateur musician and laird's protege. Eden the Atalos Indian warrior, his face proud, arrogant, slightly cruel. Naked to the waist with ornaments on his bare arms, the thunderbird around his neck with angry life shining in its eyes that seemed more than a mere trick of light.

His hair, longer than he would ever wear in an Aberdeen laboratory, tied back from his forehead by a piece of scarlet rag. Under it eyes obsidian, narrowed, watchful as a bird of prey. And the sunset wind caught at hair and scarlet rag, tugging with despairing fingers. A chill one could feel, echoing across time, for there was an entire race's anger and futile dreams in the desolation, the aching loneliness of the vast desert background where the dying rays of sunlight blazed fiercely against canyon walls.

The picture seemed bathed in blood, uneasy, frightening. It was also staggeringly good. Not a mere competent painted "photograph" nor even flattering. Alison had captured the essential personality of her sitter without which a technically sound portrait can remain a dire artistic failure. Its magnificence "cooled down" the rest of her Deeside and Aberdeen scenes, her two other portraits, into insipidity. It should never have hung in the same room with them. It belonged in a great empty space of its own.

"How do you like it?" asked Eden newly arrived, from the other side of the settee.

"Let's say it's not quite what I would want to have hanging on the dining room wall."

"What do you mean by that?" he asked, coming round to my side and regarding his almost naked image through narrowed, critical eyes.

I smiled. In the conventional gear of black suit, white shirt and dark tie, sober but elegant, there was little to identify with the savage warrior Alison had depicted.

"It's too restless. Bitter. All that desert too. Lost and alone." A *red* desert curiously enough, I thought for the first time. Like my nightmare. "Is it really you?"

He smiled and slid an arm along the back of the settee. "What a compliment," he said mockingly. "Let's say rather an atavistic portrait dreamed up by Alison's colorful imagination. As once I was, or should have been."

"She must know you extremely well. To recognize what nobody else did."

"Are you two admiring my masterpiece?" said Alison proudly.

Rosanna who had left her bearded student hobbled over and sat down heavily beside us. She gave her deep sexy chuckle. "That trick of painting more than the eye can see really came off, Alison. Reminds me of Wilde's *Picture of Dorian Gray*."

"You mean, putting characteristics into Eden from the painting instead of the other way round," said Alison in a shocked voice. "I never intended anything of the sort. What a horrible idea."

Rosanna laughed. "It's quite your best painting. But I don't think you should exhibit it with the rest of your stuff," she said candidly, expressing my own feelings, "makes 'em all look washed-out. You should stick to portraits, try that

134

trick again. Try it on Lucinda here, paint what's going on behind that pretty face – " she looked at me, smiling behind the dark glasses, "– paint in the doubts and conflicts, the memories and fears. It would be very interesting. Or try it with me, Alison, I'm an old hag now, no beauty left to insult. Perhaps none of us are what we seem. Particularly Eden," she said, regarding him thoughtfully, "Eden, who has been a cherished part of Lairigbrach so long that people are apt to forget that his background is gorier than middle-class Aberdeen."

"Aberdeen has had its moments. Remember Macbeth. Remember the Baillies who aided and abetted the slave trading in children during the seventeenth century. Remember the witch-burnings," said Eden with a shrug. "I'm not so different to the rest of you. Environment plays a much greater part in shaping characters than it is given credit for. And don't forget, when you look so admiringly at Alison's little fantasy here, that the life she depicts had been dead and forgotten for more than seventy years before I was born."

From the other side of the settee, two arms slipped around his neck, their movement followed by a cloud of perfume. "Eden darling, where have you been hiding?" asked a wounded voice.

Boredom vanished as the girl, introduced as Laura, one of Alison's students, joined us. The talk became technical and more guests arrived. As I handed out glasses of sherry and catalogues I watched Eden's head above the crowd. Occasionally I had glimpses of Laura clinging to his arm as they paused before each picture, heads close together. Eden, tall, slim and elegant, Laura, with her long dark hair, vivacious, smiling.

I remembered the first time I had seen them together in the foyer of the Music Hall when Eden played in the symphony orchestra and I was dying to know his identity. Now, as my own home had retreated into unreality, so too it seemed impossible that he had ever been the "Barbaric Stranger."

Rosanna was obviously enjoying herself without leaving her settee. I was amazed at her head for alcohol. Each time I passed by she seized another full glass, saying: "Sit down and chat for a minute, Lucinda."

I can't remember those conversations. I expect they were trivial. All I remember is that I was more interested in watching Eden and Laura with envy in my heart, until at last they disappeared. After that, as I talked to guests, to Rosanna, wherever I moved, the eyes in that unnerving portrait of Eden, followed mockingly. Like some evil monster the uncanny landscape absorbed me, so that I too felt the chilly sunset wind in my hair echoing an empty world of despair in my heart.

Chapter 13

"Can I take you up on your offer to look after the exhibition?" asked Alison next morning, throwing down an invitation to a friend's reception in Perth. "Everything happens at once. All you have to do is hand out catalogues and put stickers on any sales . . ."

"Take care of yourself," said Rosanna, as Alison let me out of the car at Holborn Junction. Rosanna inspired by yesterday's visit to the hairdresser's had decided to pick up a taxi in town and have a forage round the antique shops. Apparently there was great demand for Scots antiques in Australia – especially Orkney chairs, spinning wheels, claymores and targes.

As Alison drove away, Rosanna gave me a cheery wave. Mad about food, I wondered if her new friendliness sprang from my indulging her with a cooked breakfast.

"Kippers," she exclaimed as I took in the tray, "how did you know? I absolutely adore them." Fondness of kippers was a family failing according to the well-stocked fridge. Drew had liked kippers too and the smell of them conjured up the misery of my life with him. The homely kipper suggests a happy, wholesome family breakfast, it didn't belong in the same scene with a kinky pair like Drew and his chum Tony.

I had found Rosanna already made up that morning and I suspected, richly corseted, sitting up in bed in a voluminous wrapper. On her head an old-fashioned white frilly nightcap, which in company with the tinted glasses (slipping forward on her nose as she greedily viewed the contents of the breakfast tray), gave a startling resemblance to the Wolf who gobbled up poor Grandmama in Red Riding Hood.

Alison's students had given her a party and she had overslept. There was no response when I tapped on Eden's door. I opened it and the bed had not been slept in. No comment was made on his absence by Alison and I wondered if he had entertained Laura at his flat in town last night.

As I walked to the Art Gallery through Queen's Gardens, birds sang in the trees and with brisk determination, thrushes large and plump tapped the sunny grass and listened for worms. From the harbor a mile away, the sky echoed with the harsh excitement of seagulls wheeling against the cloudless blue. Lairigbrach seemed remote suddenly, a house seen once long ago and remembered, a story read in childhood and never forgotten.

I spent a pleasant morning studying the viewers. Some were disposed to chat but few seriously interested in buying, mostly holiday makers who came in to rest their aching feet, I suspected.

"Hello, Lucinda." And there, much to my delight was Fiona. "I phoned Lairigbrach and they told me you were here."

I had so much to tell her. First of all that the Barbaric Stranger's name was Eden Atala and he lived in Lairigbrach.

"I can't believe it. Fancy him being one of the MacAedens." Fiona listened to my story about him. "It's absolutely fantastic." When I told her about Hamish, she smiled. "You sound quite stuck on Eden. Take my advice and have Hamish instead, his family is very well-off," she added, always practical. "Your Eden sounds like a drifter. I think I'd be afraid of him," she said, looking at the portrait with a shiver.

138

She left soon afterwards to help her mother choose accessories for the wedding outfit. We would meet for lunch.

"Afraid of him." Her words seemed to linger as the darkly savage face of Eden watched me across the room from the painting. "Afraid of him."

At lunchtime, Fiona leaned across the cafe table and said in conspiratorial fashion, "Lucinda, something *is* wrong, isn't it? In the two weeks since I last saw you you're pale, drawn and just a mass of nerves. Look what you've done to that poor roll, its nothing but crumbs. What's the matter – is there something I can do?"

So I told her about the haunting, expecting her to be shocked, sympathetic, even to offer me a refuge. Instead, she leaned back, shook her head and said sadly: "Dick's been so worried about you. You know, he thought something like this might happen, that you might have hallucinations because of Drew's connection with Lairigbrach," she added triumphantly.

To my, "What rubbish," she said, "Lucinda please. We're both very fond of you." (It seemed unlikely that Dick could regard me as anything but an interesting medical case history, seeing we had only met a few times and not exchanged many more words on each occasion). "Nervous troubles are very common, you must regard it like asthma or an allergy, nothing to be ashamed of. Why not get your doctor – or Hamish – to put you on to a good psychiatrist. You've borne up wonderfully well, but these hallucinations – "

I kept calm with difficulty. "There is nothing wrong with my nerves or there wasn't until Drew – until lately."

"*We* know there's nothing *seriously* wrong," said Fiona smoothly, "but don't you understand, dear, it's like having a chest X-ray from time to time, just a safety precaution – "

"Are these two seats taken?" They weren't and two elderly ladies accompanied by numerous shopping bags, joined us. They spoke not a word to each other but maintained an avid interest in Fiona and me, their eyes fixed eagerly on whichever one of us was speaking. Such an attentive audience frustrated all conversation. Topics of weather, Edinburgh and Dick's sister were soon exhausted. Our lack of entertainment so crushed our table companions that they gathered together their sprawled belongings and departed, still wrapped in their individual icy silences.

Who were they, I wondered, fascinated by their odd behavior? But Fiona had noticed nothing unusual, concerned completely with her own world. We argued over who should pay the bill, as always, and parted with promises of "being in touch" soon.

Feeling injured and misunderstood I went back to the Gallery. Even the weather was disgruntled, thunder hung in the air, turning the grass lividly green and the birds sheltered silent in the trees, huddled in their feathers, waiting for the storm to break. The threat in the weather kept viewers down to a minimum and I had time to brood which was the last thing I needed.

Wasn't there anyone who would take me seriously about Drew? Who would believe that I had seen him? Drew is dead, said common sense. Drew is dead. Why be afraid?

Afraid of him? Afraid of him? asked the portrait of Eden each time it caught my eye. As the Gallery had no outside windows I had all the sound effects of thunder but missed rain and lightning. It was a dismal oppressing afternoon. At last with a sense of relief, I locked catalogues and sales lists in the drawer and gathering handbag and books, switched off the main strip lights above the pictures and prepared to leave.

Suddenly I noticed the figure of a man crouched on the settee near the emergency exit in the dimlylit far end of the room.

"It's closing time," I shouted. "Five-thirty." There was no response. For an embarrassing moment I wondered if he had fallen asleep. Then with a sensation of icy horror, I realized there was something terribly familiar about him.

The raincoat. Surely I had seen one like it very recently. In the cloakroom at Lairigbrach – *and it belonged to Drew*.

He rose slowly to his feet and looked straight at me. Down the length of the room I recognized the face under the deerstalker hat.

Drew!

Drew smiling, coming towards me, his hands out-stretched.

Turning I ran through the other exit to the front door. I tried to concentrate all my efforts on dragging leaden shaking limbs to the door. I tried not to faint or scream but to think coherently – and fast, on how I could escape. As I ran I thought I heard the echoing sound of footsteps behind me.

The hall was dim and in my panic, I fumbled with the lock. In the last extremity of fear, I screamed. The sound of footsteps continued. From the outside of the door.

I screamed again and suddenly the empty hall was full of people, darting out from other rooms, rushing towards me. The street door opened and I fell into Hamish's arms. "What on earth is wrong?" he asked.

"Take me away, take me away from here. Drew's in there."

"Where?"

"In the main gallery."

"What ails the lassie?" asked the janitor. "Is she hurt?"

Someone close enough to hear my cry to Hamish said, "Something about a man scaring her. Tch, tch, there's some awful folk about these days."

"Where did he go, miss?" asked the janitor.

"I don't know. Through the back exit, I think."

"You wait here," said Hamish to me, preparing to dash after the others.

141

"No, no, I'm coming with you."

The gallery was empty. The chase had ended down a small flight of steps where the basement door led into a small, walled garden and half a dozen people staring over it were shouting, "I wonder which way he went?" "See anything over your way, Jock?"

The gray backs of houses, church spires, Aberdeen suburbs decorous and dignified, their granite gleaming in the after-rain. There was nothing else.

"This man, miss, did he do – anything – to you?" asked the janitor.

"No, nothing."

The man peered at me. "Sure now? He wasna' er, misbehaving himself – anything like that, then we could get the police on to it."

"No, nothing. He just gave me a terrible fright. Somebody I used to know."

"Och, now – that's the way of it," the man grinned. "A laddie playing a practical joke on you. Well now. It's all right, you can all relax," he added to the searchers, "just a practical joker, someone the lassie knows trying to frighten her – "

"Thank you," said Hamish, and muttered to me, "Let's get out of here." He was obviously greatly embarrassed and hustled me into the car aware of the curious eyes watching us.

"I'm not mad, Hamish. I did see him. And it was Drew. Please please believe me. I did see him. I did," I shouted knowing that my hysteria made the story even less convincing.

"All right, all right," said Hamish patiently. "Here, swallow this." He thrust a small white pill into my mouth. "Now just relax. Close your eyes if you can."

I could and did. When I opened them again, I saw on the horizon the proud head of Bennachie. "This isn't the road to Lairigbrach."

"I'm taking you out country for a meal, Lucinda. We'll have a pleasant evening, good food and you can tell me all your troubles. I'll phone Eden and let him know I've kidnapped you, so stop worrying."

Clava Castle, our destination, was at its heyday when Macbeth was commuting between his Thanedoms of Fife and Cawdor, over vile roads and through blasted encounters with witches, in his own particular rat-race for the Scottish crown. Through the centuries, Clava had survived siege without and traitors within until finally after the '45, Stinking Billy Cumberland lost all patience with its defiance in sheltering Bonnie Prince Charlie, and had it laid to the sword and finished off with fire.

Now the only cries echoing along its massive ruined walls on a high hill overlooking Donside, were those of nesting birds, the only quarrels from the rookery at the Clava House Hotel, built as a mansion house in the nineteenth century and resting in a sunny hollow, sheltered by the ruined grandeur of its predecessor.

The unhappy tides of fortune had swept away three sons in World War I and without direct heirs, the house had changed owners many times and fallen into neglect, to emerge under new management some twenty years ago as a hotel, renowned for hospitality, food, and frequent reference by the gourmets of the national press.

We drove thrugh the same ancient gateway that once led to the Castle, in the footsteps of Bruce and Wallace and ill-fated Queen Mary. As we left the car, the scent of a garden after rain drifted towards us. We climbed the front steps and entered the stag-bedecked lofty hall where discreetly appetizing smells of cooking mingled with cigars and old wood panelling.

Hamish ordered me a sherry, telephoned Lairigbrach and left a message with Nurse Duncan. By the time we were shown to our table, I had already realized there was some unsubtle therapy afoot. Instead of allowing me to upset myself and spoil our evening with a wallow in my own fears, between the consommé and the Dee salmon, Hamish put me through the entire history of Clava. Battle by battle, siege by siege, one anecdote leading obligingly and engagingly to the next.

Everything reminded Hamish of a story. Much to my surprise I found myself laughing and my mood of despair vanished, its place taken by one of reckless gaiety, partially induced by excellent food and wine. Somewhere between the crepe suzette and the coffee with Drambuie, a very clear picture of Dr Hamish Faro emerged.

I saw him as a middle-class boy, a doctor's son, who had spent all his life in Aberdeen, had entered Robert Gordon's College at five, as his father and grandfather before him, and maintaining an average career with some special distinction on the sports field, had proceeded in due course to Aberdeen University.

An uncomplicated, down-to-earth lowland Scot, average in everything but looks. A born raconteur but luckily lacking the intense imagination that would make his choice of profession an agonizing thousand deaths per day, romance would be tempered with caution and generosity with a keen eye to value obtained. He would never throw his bonnet over the windmill or covet his neighbor's wife, but would please his family by marrying some nice average middle-class girl so that in due course the conventional middle-class dynastic pattern would be assured.

Suddenly the bill was being paid, Hamish reminding me that he was "on call" after nine that evening. My mood changed, all gaiety vanished as the cold wind of terror hurled open the sanctuary of the cozy hotel lounge. I could picture Lairigbrach already lurking, waiting for me, sinister and dark against the sky, with the hills folded down to sleep across the river.

"I don't want to go back," I said to Hamish as I followed him to the car. "What if Drew is there waiting?"

144

His smile vanished. He took my hand and studied it silently for a moment. "Lucinda, you don't believe all this nonsense about ghosts, do you – an intelligent girl like you?" When I didn't answer, he said, "Drew is dead. Unquestionably, absolutely dead and gone. There are no such things as ghosts," he explained, kindly, gently, like someone consoling a frightened child after a bad dream. "All this ESP that's so fashionable just now, everyone is out looking for psychic experiences – it's all in their imagination, you know. You couldn't get me to believe a word of it, not in a thousand years. There simply has to be a scientific explanation for everything. If you accept ghosts, then you take the lot – spiritualism, reincarnation, black magic – you put civilization right back into the Dark Ages – "

I listened unconvinced. A week ago I would have agreed with him but now I just wasn't sure. "If I didn't see Drew, then *who did* I see?"

"Look, Lucinda, you're in a bad state of nerves. Right? Well, a man wearing a checked raincoat, a hat similar to one Drew had, perhaps the same type and height and because you're hung up on the idea of him haunting you, you superimpose his face on to a stranger."

"Then why did he walk towards me?" I asked, shuddering as I remembered the hands outstretched, the taunting, smiling face in the dim light of the gallery.

"I imagine he was some ordinary man, simply wanting to ask you an innocent question about one of the pictures. He came towards you, you rushed out, began to scream – "

"Then why did he vanish?"

Hamish smiled indulgently. "My dear girl, in similar circumstances, most men would. Alone in a gallery with a hysterical woman who starts screaming as you did, as if she'd met Frankenstein. Most men, myself included, would have taken to their heels and got away fast before some very awkward explanations were necessary. Supposing you had said he was molesting you? You obviously got the significance of the way the janitor's mind was running?

"After all," he reminded me gently, "the other night at Lairigbrach you went into hysterics because you saw Eden walking in the garden and somehow the moonlight made you think you were seeing Drew, although there isn't the slightest resemblance between them. Couldn't that kind of illusion have happened this time?"

"The time in the garden was different. I agree moonlight could have distorted what I saw. But the man in the art gallery was definitely Drew. For heaven's sake, Hamish, I know Drew – I was married to him, I couldn't mistake anyone else for him – "

"Yes, you could. In moonlight, or in dim-light if you were in a highly suggestible state emotionally. Believe me, these fantasies of the imagination are common symptoms of a guilt complex." He looked at me hesitantly, and switched on the engine. The car slid smoothly down the drive, out of the stone gateway. "I don't want to pry into your affairs but I gather it was an unhappy marriage, followed by a separation."

"Yes." He waited politely for me to enlarge on the details but again I was tongue-tied at the prospect of discussing the gruesome details of my life with Drew.

"There you are," he said triumphantly, "an unhappy marriage, followed by a separation. The partner dies and naturally someone as sensitive as yourself starts to think – if I hadn't left him would he still be alive – "

I stopped listening. There wasn't a word of reality in it – or hope for me, from beginning to end. Hamish couldn't have been further from the truth that was somewhere just under our noses. Sometimes I felt I had it within my grasp, the right explanation, the solution –

And a thought cold as ice touched my heart.

"If I'm not being haunted," I interrupted, "you know much more about Eden and the MacAedens than I do. Suppose someone – at Lairigbrach – is behind it. Can you think of any reason why they should want to play a trick like this on me – especially as they all deny that they want anything out of Lairigbrach when Elliott dies? All of them protest that it would be a millstone around their necks – "

"Good heavens," said Hamish indignantly, "a trick. Only a madman would play a trick like that. Hold on."

The car skidded through deep mud in the narrow lane. For a few moments Hamish was absorbed in getting it righted, then the rain began again, falling like stair-rods and reducing visibility to nil. Hamish peered through the windshield wipers unable to cope with the streams of water. They jerked back and forward spasmodically and in the silence that filled the car they whispered: "Madman, madman, madman . . ."

Hamish was silent until we reached the main road. I had offended him, for he began a defensive account of Eden, how kind, how good, illustrated with small moral examples of his goodness and kindness throughout the years.

I listened politely. Driving carefully in fierce conditions, Hamish reached the North Deeside Road. A few minutes later the car nosed down the drive, with the storm in full flood.

There was Lairigbrach almost obliterated by great sheets of rain. It looked dead and deserted, a haunted house from a poor television picture, gray, grainy and unreal.

Hamish kissed me goodnight with enthusiasm that would have appealed greatly in happier circumstances and I dashed up the front steps convinced as I did so that Lairigbrach might disappear and the credit titles appear.

As I grasped the door handle a great flash of lightning illuminated the sky and the trees stood on tiptoe, a herd of strange monsters with green heads, huddled together as if for protection, wondering which of their number was marked down for destruction.

I went into the hall and thunder roared overhead, rattling the windows of the house. I closed the door thankfully. But the storm without was more than equalled by the storm within, where terror and hysterics raked the air.

I was no longer in danger of madness, or alone in my hallucinations.

Someone else had seen Drew . . .

Chapter 14

The latest victim was Alison.

"I found her in a dead faint at the foot of the stairs, the poor thing," whispered Rosanna dramatically. "Nurse Duncan gave her a sedative."

"How did it happen?"

Alison looked out of the drawing-room window apprehensively. "TeeDee had been in all day. She was in the kitchen in her basket, so I decided to take her for a walk across the lawns. Then she disappeared. I called her and nothing happened. Then I heard her yelp – "

Anxiously I held her closer, as she nestled in my arms.

"Don't worry," said Rosanna, "she wasn't hurt, only frightened. The little pet, there now. Come to Rosanna." I put her on the settee and she immediately snuggled in between the two women, looking more scared, I thought, than either of them.

"Anyway," Alison continued, "she came out of the bushes as if the devil himself was behind her, then – " she took a deep breath, "– I saw – Drew – walking quickly towards the house. From the direction of the old kirkyard. It *was* Drew. He had on that checked raincoat and the deerstalker hat – " She mistook my startled cry for one of incredibility and said defiantly, "I tell you I *saw* him. It was broad daylight and I have excellent eyesight."

"What time?" I whispered.

"Oh, I'm not absolutely certain. I got home from Perth about six. Sometime after that – "

And I had seen him at five-thirty in the Art Gallery. There was little point in adding to their fears by telling them that. Neither of them were in the right mood to appreciate a certain strange significance in the haunting

"I'll never forget it," said Rosanna, clutching TeeDee closer as if for comfort. "I was in my room and I heard this scream. Then footsteps running through into the hall. I looked over the banister and there was Alison lying quite still at the bottom of the stairs. I had a terrible fright, you know. I'm much too old for this sort of thing," she added reproachfully.

"He was right behind me," said Alison, her eyes glazed like someone in shock. "Oh, Lucinda, it was awful. He came after me into the house. I could even hear his breathing, I tell you."

(That was interesting, I thought, do ghosts usually breathe?)

Rosanna shook her head, "Thought you were dead, Alison. By the time I fetched my stick and hobbled downstairs, naturally there wasn't anyone in sight. Not that I expected there would be." She leaned across and clasped Alison's hand. "You know what has brought all this about, don't you? I warned you. It's that ouija board. God only knows what elementals we've released. If you know a professional medium in Aberdeen, we'd better get help – and soon."

"I'll make some coffee. Coming, TeeDee?" But TeeDee wagged her stump of tail apologetically and declined my invitation. Rosanna stroked her head. "She's such an affectionate little soul," she said smiling up at me. "Seems to have taken a fancy to old Rosanna. All animals do, you know."

Nurse Duncan came into the kitchen. "Funny business, yonder. Seeing ghosts, whatever next? I was having a rest in my little room, so I really didn't hear much from downstairs," (as her room was the former dressing-room attached to Elliott's bedroom, it wasn't surprising). "First I heard was the old girl shrieking blue murder and there was Miss Grantly lying in a heap. Ghosts, hmm?" she said in disgust. "Lot of nonsense, I'm sure there's a perfectly logical explanation for it all, but all the same I'll be glad to get out of this house, I can tell you."

"How's your patient?"

"Just the same, just the same. He could linger like this for ages, if you ask me. Must have a real strong core. Thank goodness the other nurse takes over next week. I'll be glad of a spell, really I will. We all thought it was just for a few days," she whispered significantly, departing with her tray.

A perfectly logical explanation for it all, Nurse Duncan had said. As I made coffee I was amazed at how coldly, calmly I could view it – now that I knew for certain there was no ghost.

Drew was certainly dead and gone, but for some reason, a pretense was being made, first to me, then to Alison, that his ghost was haunting us. As I put biscuits on a plate, I wondered had I been the only victim intended? Was it just a mistake that Alison had seen him? All the evidence pointed to an inhabitant of Lairigbrach as the culprit.

Who then could be immediately discounted? Elliott, Nurse Duncan, Rosanna. I had mistaken both Alison and Eden at different times for Drew, for all three were of the same height and build. Now Alison was eliminated. She was a poor actress, I suspected, and her fear seemed genuine.

So that left only – Eden. As the cold trickle of fear chilled me to the bone, I wondered why I hadn't insisted that Hamish take me back to the safety of John Knox Avenue that night. No one, certainly not Pearl, would have resented my presence after such a terrifying experience and Dad would have insisted that I leave Lairigbrach immediately.

151

With painful suddenness I realized why I had wanted to be here in Lairigbrach. The kitchen door opened and there was my reason. And I ran into his arms blindly like a forest creature to its nest.

"Hello, hello. What's all this in aid of?" he asked smiling.

"Eden, something dreadful has happened. I saw Drew this afternoon at the Art Gallery. And now Alison has seen him here, in the garden – "

He listened but didn't seem surprised. "Look, Hamish told me about your encounter, when I saw him a few minutes ago." He paused frowning. "Alison too, eh?"

"I suppose Hamish told you it was all hallucination, my guilt complex. All very smoothly explained by medical science. Oh, don't deny it, I can see you're quite convinced – "

He put an arm around me. "Of course I wasn't, sweetie. Alison's apparition seems to confirm that something distinctly odd is going on, but whether it's supernatural or not – I keep an open mind on such matters. Here, let me carry that."

I followed him into the drawing room and sat beside Rosanna on the settee, while TeeDee overcome with canine loyalty shifted her position to rest her head on my knee. As I handed round coffee and listened to Alison's replies to Eden's calm questions, I tried this second time over to get the clue that had eluded me in Alison's minute details. Was her story all an elaborate pretense? Had I been foolish to dismiss her so readily as a suspect? After all once I had mistaken her for Drew in a dim light? She was more like him than any of the legitimate MacAedens.

Conversation was like a rat trapped in a cage, frantically scuttling back and forth over the same tiny area. Finally Eden persuaded them both to go to bed and Rosanna offered Alison a sleeping pill, with the cheering words:

"I'm afraid you've brought all this about yourself, my

dear. The ouija board can be very dangerous in inexperienced hands, especially if there is a restless spirit in the house. We must get a medium, a reliable one and have a seance. It's the only way. There's somebody here," she looked round us all and though her eyes were innocent, smiling, they lingered on me for just a fraction too long, I thought, "there's somebody here who wished Drew ill – and now he wants vengeance."

"Rubbish," said Eden. "Drew's dead and nothing can change that."

Rosanna gave him an angry look. "I think we need people here who loved him and can persuade him to rest in peace." She sighed. "I wonder if I could get hold of that nice young friend of his, Tony. I had a postcard from him before I left home – he's on tour in the Midlands at the moment. If only I could remember where – such a nuisance, I'm sure I could have persuaded him to come to Lairigbrach for a weekend. He was a great admirer of mine," she said, preening herself a little.

I was certain that Tony would have found other elderly ladies to admire by now and other chums too. Drew would be just a name, one among many. However the prospect of ever seeing him again was only a little less chilling than the ghost of his monstrous friend.

Eden returned from seeing the ladies safely upstairs. "There's one obvious answer to all this. Has anyone checked whether Drew's coat is still in the cloakroom? If anyone wore it, the chances are with a day like this, it's probably damp."

In the cloakroom he dragged it from the back of the cupboard. "No. Bone dry. Wait a minute. Feel that." Crawling with revulsion I touched one sleeve. There was a wet patch on the elbow. The hat had been pushed to the back of the shelf. "Distinctly damp," said Eden, "perhaps that convinced you that you're not a victim of

153

the supernatural. Ghosts don't hang up wet raincoats on hangers before they dematerialize."

He opened the front door. In the strange light of a northern summer where there is no darkness, a solitary blackbird poured out its sweet melancholy into eternal twilight. Somewhere an owl hooted lazily in a rain-washed world, refreshed, reborn.

Eden put his arm around my shoulders. I looked at him, hoping the night would conceal what I knew and could no longer hide from myself. For in that moment of silent communication it seemed impossible that I had ever considered Eden might well be the evil genius of Lairigbrach, at work on some deadly game of his own to destroy me.

"Still frightened, Lucy?"

"Not in the slightest."

"Good girl." He smiled down at me. "From what Hamish told me you were at breaking-point. This is a surprising change."

"I was at breaking-point because I thought I was being haunted by Drew. Now I know there's a human agency at work behind the scenes, I'm prepared to fight back. I assure you, nothing is going to drive me away from Lairigbrach until I find out who's behind it all."

"Good for you, Lucy. We'll fight them together. Suspect anyone?" he asked casually.

"It can't be Elliott, Nurse Duncan or Rosanna. But it could be Alison if she was trying to throw me off the scent."

"True. But I don't think so." He paused, then said heartily, "There's someone you've missed." I didn't reply. "Me, Lucy," he said, his dark eyes gleaming. "You know damned well you've thought it could be me. After all you did mistake me for him right at the beginning."

"I was still asleep. The moonlight plays tricks. I know it isn't you." I laughed but its false sound didn't convince either of us. "What do you think?" I asked hastily.

154

"That there must be a simple explanation – logical or diabolical." He locked the door on the magic garden, switched off the lights and we went upstairs together. Happy and safe encircled by his arm, I would have agreed to any suggestion he made, concerning Drew's haunting or matters much closer to my heart at that moment.

"On happier topics," he said, "Gillian's sister and her boy-friend are up from St Andrew's and she wants to celebrate by taking them for a barbecue to my beach. Just a few friends. How about coming? I stopped by to invite Hamish. Like to go with him?" On the dark landing he smiled. "Hamish's quite hung up on you. I suppose you've realized that. You're a lucky girl, he's a fine fellow – "

There's nothing quite so diminishing or unflattering for a girl than being handed over on a silver platter by the man who really interests her, to his very best friend. I remembered Hamish at that first dance where I saw Eden, getting rid of me to his red-headed chum so that he could take Fiona home alone. Fiona who so soon transferred her affections to Dick. Now with exquisite irony, the wheel had turned again.

"Goodnight, Lucy." His kiss lingered. Then I was alone in Janet's room, her picture smiling at me, from a world where her own joys and sorrows had long since departed. I remembered I must ask Eden about the painting of Atala which Alison had deposited with an art expert friend for restoring and framing.

As we walked down the steep cliff path to Eden's beach, the day was still warm although the sun had gone, leaving a lavender sea. There were ten of us and Hamish held my hand all the time, making a great show of devotion. I suspected this was for Fiona's special benefit, proving that he hadn't been too sadly afflicted by her desertion.

Fiona and Dick had been invited that morning. I was elbow deep in filing papers in Elliott's study when Fiona telephoned. Could they take me out for a Chinese meal? She was delighted to join our party instead.

"I'm just dying to meet this Eden of yours," she said.

After the barbecued steaks, the crisp rolls and wine, the sky had darkened and the sea frozen into silver. Only the rocks crouched black and shining, and as some of the guests rested against them after dancing to the transistor radio, cigarettes glowed as if sleeping monsters had opened small red eyes and closed them hastily again.

The dancing grew closer, more abandoned, the laughter wilder. Fiona and Dick clung together aloof and a little distrustful, armored in the respectability of approaching marriage. Someone asked Eden to play the guitar. Stripped to the waist, the firelight showing harsh planes of cheekbone and mouth, his downbent head absorbed and dedicated, turned back the time a hundred years. Alison's portrait of "The Warrior" was suddenly alive. At last he said, "No more, no more" and switched on the radio.

He sprang up, came over to my side and ignoring Hamish said, "Dance with me, Lucy." I wore only a thin mini-dress, bare-armed, bare-necked. His naked chest, the warm face against my own, brought a nearness, an intimacy as if we were one flesh. The music over, he let me go slowly and I saw the look in his eyes and he still held my hands.

In that illuminating moment, I knew how much I loved him. I stood on shifting sands where tomorrow the piper must be paid, the price perhaps my immortal soul. And every instinct cried out that I mustn't let it happen. If I had to fall in love, then it must not be with one of the MacAedens.

There were light footsteps beside us. Gillian threw her arms around him, kissed his mouth. "Faithless type," she whispered. "You don't mind if I take him away, do you?" she asked me rather coldly.

156

Watching them on the fringe of the firelight, talking earnestly, heads close together, hand-in-hand and oblivious of us all was too painful a sight. I turned away but Hamish was already at my side, where he had been all evening, apart from that one dreamlike interlude with Eden and a couple of rather silent duty dances with Dick. As we mingled with the other guests I felt as if I had lived for ever and watched it all before, through so many different eyes. Love and lust and trust – the pattern of an ancient story too often told.

But as always with Hamish, blank despair and the hollow ache disappeared before his comforting ability to make me laugh. Once I saw Eden stop talking to Gillian, raise his head and look at us as our laughter drifted over to him. I pretended not to notice and gave all my attention to Hamish, grateful that he was so refreshingly ordinary and uncomplicated. And like memory handled across a great gulf of years, I remembered that only last week I had found him extremely attractive and imagined I might fall in love with him.

We walked away from the others towards the cave. In its shadows he kissed me with such hunger and intensity, I knew the words could not be withheld.

"I love you, Lucinda." When I didn't answer, he said gently, "I was hoping you felt the same way."

"I like you very much, Hamish. You're a good friend." I put my hand on his arm, taking refuge in a lie so ancient, so insincere that it hurt. "I have to get my emotions sorted out. After one unhappy marriage, I need a lot of time – "

"There is hope then."

A few yards away Eden leaned on one elbow, smiling at Gillian, and I knew there was no hope. Because I loved him. Now as we joined the others I cursed a destiny that made falling in love in phase an impossibility for me. If it had happened that night at the dance when I was so desperately unhappy and Hamish had eyes only for Fiona, then we too might have been dreaming of a lifetime together. And Eden? Eden would be only a dark face vividly remembered and my little world would be safe from invasion by the MacAedens.

As we drove back to town and Hamish smiled at me, I wondered what strange chemistry made my wayward heart choose a complex man like Eden, who by his own admission didn't know the meaning of being in love, who loathed all possible strings and would run a mile if any girl tried to marry him. Worst of all, he was possibly related to Drew – "the near in blood, the nearer bloody." Association with Lairigbrach was developing bad habits, the family failing of a quotation from *Macbeth* for every emergency.

We went to Eden's flat in Old Aberdeen. Two rambling high-ceilinged rooms on a Queen Anne house in the Chanonry, property of the University. It suited Eden. With black leather suite, saffron walls and white wood-work, crowded bookshelves, some modern paintings and pieces of pottery, it had charm and dignity, the personal touches that reduced his room at Lairigbrach to a mere monastic cell.

I was surprised (and Fiona a little shocked) that Gillian was so much at home. Obviously she had made herself at home on many previous occasions. While I was combing my hair in the bedroom she came in, opened a drawer here and there and shouted, "Eden darling, where did you put my earrings?"

Eden detached himself from the group by the record player.

"I got a terrible row from Mother – they're hers really," she said.

He opened a cigarette box. "Here they are. I rescued them."

"From where?" she asked coyly.

"I think that is rather classified information, Gillian, or would you like our friend here to know?"

She snatched them from him with a delighted shriek and dashed into the kitchen. "If you're going to be indelicate, I'd better make coffee."

Eden went out avoiding my eyes. Presumably when he was offering me sanctuary in the flat the other night, it still had an inmate. I was amazed at the fury of my jealousy and indignation that he should want us both. Then I realized that he had offered me only a refuge and that he didn't want any woman on a permanent basis. His way with many was simply an escape clause, the guard against serious involvement with one.

We had coffee. Gillian sat on Eden's knee. Hamish and I danced to the record player, but I had no heart in it. I was tired, sick of being here. I wanted desperately to go home – wherever that was. Some of them dashed off to a late dance at Marischal College and I was thankful that Hamish, officially "on call" this evening had found a substitute only until midnight. When she heard this, a pretty little nurse who knew him from the hospital (and had been eyeing him all evening), asked for a lift as she lived in the next road and was on early duty tomorrow morning.

Hamish, rather embarrassed, gave me a questioning look.

"That's fine Hamish," said Eden. "I'll take Lucy home. Get your coat, Gillian, we'll drop you on the way."

"But – " she protested, giving me a furious look.

As Fiona and I went hastily into the bedroom to collect our coats, I heard him say, "Come on, Gillian, don't make a fuss. There'll be other nights."

"Weird set-up this," said Fiona. "I thought you told me he lived in Lairigbrach. A right love-nest. I think you should let Hamish take you home. That nurse is making a play for him." But Hamish had gone.

In the kitchen Gillian had her arms around Eden's neck. "I'll stay if you'll come back. Get rid of her. How about that?" she whispered.

Eden shook his head. "No. Not tonight. I'm weary. I want an early night. If you're still feeling energetic, why not go with the gang?"

"I damned well will at that," she said angrily and brushing past me without a word, dashed out after the others.

I followed Eden to the car and he drove without speaking. He looked drained, tired to death. Soon we were speeding through the suburbs along Great Western Road and down the drive to Lairigbrach. He didn't usually drive this fast.

"Is something wrong?" I asked.

He glanced at me. "'By the pricking of my thumbs . . .' Geese on my grave . . . I just don't know – "

But seconds later we both knew. When we found my poor TeeDee poisoned in the kitchen.

Chapter 15

The first thing we discovered was that the kitchen door wouldn't open. TeeDee was wedged behind it. She had got that far in a last valiant bid to die with those humans she loved before the poison took effect.

Eden pushed, pushed again. And a small mass of black wool dislodged slithered limply across the floor. From far away I heard myself scream.

Eden picked her up and laid her limp body on the table. I watched helplessly, waiting for him to reassure me, tell me it wasn't real. It hadn't happened and TeeDee couldn't be dead. That quiet boneless little body would bark and run and leap into my arms again with frantic joy.

There was a patch of sickness on the floor, a piece of uneaten chicken. "Poisoned meat," said Eden. "We have a chance. She's still alive – just. Luckily she has a dainty appetite and takes her time eating."

"But why – Eden, why should anyone? – "

"Clear out, Lucy. There's a good girl." He rolled up his sleeves.

"I want to stay."

"And I don't want you here. I've only got minutes, it isn't pretty. She may die. Now will you go. Go. And don't waste my time arguing."

I went upstairs dragging my legs like an old woman. I wanted to tell someone, share my terror and fear, but it was too late, the house in darkness, Rosanna who loved TeeDee, and Alison asleep, unaware of what had happened. I sat by the bedroom window, expecting to wait for hours and Eden came up so quickly after me, carrying TeeDee absurdly small with her lolling head, I was sure she must have died.

"I've done all I can," he said. "I hope we were in time. I've made her sick again and the Boss always kept a poison antidote after we lost one of his Labradors the same way."

I touched her timidly and she didn't move.

"Who did it, Eden? Who's want to kill a harmless little thing like her?"

"I thought you might have the answer to that. The meat was slipped through the back door."

"By someone who knew chicken was her special favorite."

Eden looked grim. "Chicken is a sure bet with most dogs, Lucy."

I spread her blanket on the bed and as he laid her gently on it, that absurd stump of tail gave a tiny quiver of recognition. Eden sat down and stroked her stomach, murmuring softly to her, words I didn't know.

"Is that a magic spell? Please God, make it a magic spell."

Eden looked up at me, his smile crooked. "Sorry, in extremes I'm apt to revert to my old gods. They're approachable, full of weaknesses and strengths like the human beings they were patterned on. I think they'd understand even a scrap of a dog's need for magic."

"How did you know what to do with her? If we'd been minutes later – "

He smiled. "Didn't they tell you that as descendant of the Sun-God of the Atalos, I'm also a medicine man in my own right? A family failing, passed on by great-grandfather Atala." He looked at TeeDee, his face serious again. "Curiously enough, I had encountered this one before, in this very house and having the antidote from last time

162

– what's more, knowing where to find it. Just the other day I was searching in that cupboard for some ink remover . . . I only hope it hasn't lost its potency." He sighed, his eyes weary. "I've done all I can, believe me. All we do now is hope – or pray."

"Which god do you pray to, Eden?"

He shrugged, still stroking TeeDee. "The Sun God or Jesus Christ – who knows. Maybe they're all one and the same in the end, the Givers of Life? Anyway, neither one will let the bastard who did this vile thing go unpunished."

But who had it been? Someone – a stranger? And despite my bravery of yesterday when I had come to terms with the idea that I was being tricked, the thought of Drew's ghost gliding across the lawns from the old kirkyard came surging back. Drew with hatred in his heart, conjured up from the grave like a zombie by Alison's ouija board.

As if he knew my thoughts, Eden said: "You have to be something of a sadist for a job like dog-poisoning."

"Did they discover who poisoned Elliott's dog?"

"No. But I had my suspicions. Drew was here at the time. He was tormenting her and she bit him. He swore death and bloody vengeance. But Elliott would never believe ill of Drew. So an unknown poacher, someone with a grudge against Lairigbrach was blamed. But I never had the slightest doubt – it was Drew all right." He continued stroking TeeDee, lips moving, eyes closed, as though he could will her to live.

I wanted to cry out loud. This was the man I loved and love was a runaway snowball on a downhill slope. Every passing hour it grew, gathering momentum. What hopes and dreams would be shattered when I reached the end of the journey and found that he could never love me in return.

Without looking up, he asked, "What in dear heaven's

163

name was a nice girl like you doing with a man like that? As for marrying him . . ."

"I had an excellent reason. The baby."

"I'd forgotten. Poor Lucy. Candidly I wouldn't have thought him capable or interested in fatherhood. Good grief girl, surely you knew – did you ever meet friend Tony?"

"I did indeed. Too late to discover Drew had married me – one reason anyway – to spite Tony who was the better actor and had got a part in a Broadway play without him. The other reason, that I learned from Elliott when we first met, was to provide an heir for Lairigbrach and secure his own inheritance. When Tony came back I was in the early stages of pregnancy, nauseated most of the time, disinterested in sex. This didn't suit Drew at all. He wanted to use me to prove to Tony that he could switch whenever he liked. So he started giving me drugs, and Tony too. Taunting him – until – until – "

"Go on," said Eden grimly.

"'There's Lucy,' he said, 'my own delectable Lucy. Yours for the taking – a pretty experiment with my blessing, Tony boy. We've always shared everything. I wouldn't deny you her too.' I tried to run away from them, but they locked me in my bedroom, tied me to the bed – " Somehow I found the words to go on, to re-live those days and nights of horror, the words I'd never found for the scenes I had buried so deeply they only erupted in nightmares.

"Stop it, stop it," said Eden and held my head against his shoulder shutting away that other world with its hideous memories. "My God, I could kill him, I could cut him into small pieces, if only for that."

"Let me finish, Eden. There isn't much more. Once I stopped fighting, they let me go. Maybe they got bored. But I ran away, I had the baby and he died. And I was glad, glad because he might have grown up to be like Drew."

164

Eden took my face gently in his hands and when they came away wet, I hadn't realized until then, that I could still cry, not even for my little TeeDee. "Thank you for making me human again," I said and he kissed my mouth. Between us TeeDee stirred, gave a whimper and wagged her ridiculous tail.

We gave her a drink of water, but she was still weak standing like a new-born lamb with splaying, wobbly legs.

Eden put her into my arms, bent down and took off my shoes and sat me back against the pillows. "Curl up and go to sleep, Lucy. She'll live."

"Don't leave me," I said.

"I have no intentions of leaving you. This bed is indecently large for one. I think we can share it, chaperoned by TeeDee. Or do we need it?" He lifted TeeDee gently into her basket and took me in his arms.

Towards morning I awoke with my head on his shoulder. From the portrait Janet smiled, a pale ghost, but happy for us both. And with the strange certainty of a waking dream I knew that somewhere she too had rested her head in the arms of a man who wore, like Eden, a thunderbird around his neck, glistening with cold eyes in the early dawn.

Before we slept, Eden said, "You're both going to the flat tomorrow, you're not spending another day in Lairigbrach. And on the way to Old Aberdeen we're calling in at the Registrars to make arrangements to be married."

"Eden, please, it doesn't have to be as final as that. After all, it's one thing being sorry for someone, quite another marrying – "

"Sorry for you. Do you really think after this night between us I'm marrying you out of pity, to take care of you. My darling girl, make no mistake about it. I'm marrying you because I need you. I've loved girls but I never needed anyone until you came along. I love you and I need you – to make me complete."

165

Eden awoke and kissed me. And morning was a great sunlit frame with a cluster of birds singing in one corner. "Love isn't always cruel, Lucy. It can be gentle and kind too." And it was just as he said.

The occupants of Lairigbrach were horrified at the story of TeeDee's narrow escape. Rosanna was mildly hysterical and clutched TeeDee in her arms as if to protect her from further onslaughts of poisoners and the air at the breakfast table was thick with speculation as Alison remembered the last time. "I wonder if it was poachers again."

When Eden announced that we were getting married both were unstinting in their congratulations but when he added that I was leaving Lairigbrach immediately, they wailed: "Oh, she can't do that. We're having the seance tonight. You must stay for that . . . Please, Lucinda. Mrs Bosquay is fixed for eight o'clock."

"Mrs Bosquay. That old charlatan," said Eden. "She's just a fairground fortune-teller – "

"That's a lie," said Alison. "Just because some of her seances went wrong."

"Or were pushed," said Eden grimly. He looked at us all. "I'm warning you, if you're seriously thinking of tampering with the supernatural in this house, have some second thoughts. Too many things have happened here."

"I didn't know you were interested," said Alison.

"I suppose its the old Indian gods that won't let him go." Rosanna smiled. "Perhaps we can get Mrs Bosquay to tell us what the future holds for Lucinda, if she's a fortune-teller."

I took Eden's hand. "No, thank you. I'd rather wait and see."

"Of course, I forgot. Alison tells me you're psychic but you won't co-operate. She saw strange things in your hand."

I was prepared to dismiss even that – my red desert

166

dream which Alison had seen so plainly, as the one disquieting inexplicable evidence of the supernatural which practically all people, however unimaginative, experience at some time. A dream that comes true – once. The premonition of a loved one's death – or danger – Once. But to be habitually in receipt of such communications would be a highly uncomfortable business, fraught with terror. I thought of professional mediums as slightly dotty like Madame Arcarti in "Blithe Spirit".

"All right, we'll both stay. Two skeptics at your grisly feast," said Eden.

Nurse Duncan waved us conspiratorially into the kitchen. "Don't have anything to do with it," she warned. "Old Bosquay is well known. She'll conjure up anyone from Cleopatra to your Uncle Joe for a good fee and a briefing beforehand. And mark my words, those two are up to something, they've been phoning back and forth. She knows all about Drew by now. I'm surprised at two well-educated ladies like them," she said with a disapproving nod in the direction of the drawing-room, "being party to a nasty little fraud."

When Eden and I were alone, I said, "I wish you hadn't agreed."

He frowned. "I want to see them confounded. Mrs Bosquay *is* a fraud, but I want to see how she works it. Don't worry, I intend to keep an eye on that table and I can move to a light switch quicker than any of you."

"But what – if it is – Drew . . ."

"Drew is dead. His power over you has gone for ever. You must start believing that, my darling. If there's anything going on at Lairigbrach it's the living behind it not the dead. And I want to know who, before we leave here for ever." He stroked my hair. "Tonight nothing can harm you, because I love you and love is stronger than evil – "

Nothing can harm you. And I believed him – then. But as the day progressed and the hours fled in the normal things of life, I recognized a sense of dread, a sick fear of the unknown like someone having an anaesthetic for the first time.

At eight o'clock, Eden drew the thick curtains across the drawing-room windows and lit the candles at Alison's request. Eden had offered to help her prepare the room so that he "could keep an eye on what they were up to."

"I intend to sit very near the light switches," he said to me.

The clock hadn't finished striking when Mrs Bosquay arrived. She came straight into the drawing room sniffing the air like a nervous deer. "We're in luck, Alison," she said. "They're with us tonight."

We took our seats round the small circular table. Rosanna and Alison, with Mrs Bosquay between them. She explained, "I need the sensitives, the believers close to me, as it helps vibrations."

I sat next to Eden, with Alison on my left, Rosanna on his right. The three women fussed and chatted, twitching at cardigans and smoking what they called their "last cigarettes." Eden whispered, "What a trio. Now we know what Macbeth had to contend with when he encountered their predecessors at Endor . . ."

Mrs Bosquay was large, extremely fat and looked as if she thrived more on foods for the table than foods for the spirit. A comfortable, sentimental, good-humored housewife, the kind one met in the supermarket every day, her only involvement in mankind, the joys and sorrows of her family. She looked less like a medium than I could ever have imagined.

Alison, large-boned, untidy, colorless – the picture of a practical no-nonsense spinster. Both were outshone by Rosanna, grotesquely vivid, down to the last false eyelash and the luxuriant blonde hair which didn't quite match the rather coarse face beneath.

And on my other side, Eden. In profile like an avenging

high priest from an old Aztec painting, the knife held high ready to strike. I shuddered. The Mad MacAedens and their friends. Out in full force one could visualize a re-enactment of Macbeth without severely overtaxing the imagination.

Mrs Bosquay put out her cigarette and was patiently explaining what we might expect, smiling and pleasant, unafraid and undramatic as a demonstrator at a cookery course. "If I go into trance, please don't any of you touch me. It could be dangerous as I will be out of my body. Now let us join hands."

"Is there anyone there?" she repeated the question slowly, patiently, several times. Nothing happened. She looked apologetically at our disbelieving faces and said, "Sometimes the spirits are slow in warming up. They even sulk. It takes a while to get – "

Under our joined hands the table jerked violently. "Here we go," said Eden, "keep watching."

"Who are you? Are you Drew MacAeden?" asked Alison. While we waited for a reply, she nodded in Mrs Bosquay's direction, who was lolling back in her chair, eyes closed. "Going into trance," Alison mouthed at us.

"Drew. Yes, of course I'm Drew. Who else?" And even knowing it was all trickery, I was still rooted with fear, for the imitation of Drew's mocking drawling tones was superb. How on earth did Mrs Bosquay manage that?

"We are your friends," said Alison slowly. "We want to help you to rest."

"Friends," said Drew's voice. "All but two. The woman who longed for my death, who never loved me and is here to get Lairigbrach for herself. The other, her lover. Betrayed, betrayed by them both," the voice moaned.

A charlatan maybe, but an impressive performance especially as Mrs Bosquay appeared to be asleep, her head sunk on her chest. She must also be a ventriloquist of considerable talent. I was thankful Nurse Duncan had warned me –

"Friends?" queried the voice again. Alison looked at me guiltily, licked dry lips. "What would you have us do so that you can find peace?"

I wished they would hurry, get it over with. The room was growing colder, colder by the second, my teeth chattering in spite of the fire. Surely the temperature after a warm summer's day should never have dropped this quickly. And everything was so still. The firelight, the candles gleaming but unmoving. I tried to turn my hand in Eden's but nothing happened. I looked round the table at the others.

They were completely motionless, like a still taken from a film as if all time had frozen and this room with its occupants had been turned to stone. There was no noise outside the room either, no clocks ticked, no quiver of sound from the garden –

Then filling the silence, echoing round the walls came another voice, "Eden Atala, Eden Atala. Do you hear me?"

From a thousand miles away, Eden answered, "I hear."

The voice, deeper than Eden's or Drew's, spoke in another language, a hissing, spitting, rasping torrent of words. Mrs Bosquay hadn't moved. It seemed incredible that this was part of the fraud, that she should have the strength for this voice, strangely terrible yet – oddly familiar. I had heard it before, but where?

Suddenly Drew's voice again, "My throat, take your hands off me. Let me alone . . . You're choking me."

He screamed and Rosanna struggled to her feet and took hold of Mrs Bosquay's shoulders. "There's someone there. Someone behind her. Can't any of you see him. For God's sake, he's strangling her. Stop him – " She seized Mrs Bosquay who cried out in a thin terrible wail and slumped

170

back in her chair, a purple-faced rag-doll, convulsed and dreadful.

And whatever had been in the room with us was gone. Warmth returned, firelight moved, candles fluttered in a draught. And the garden, as Eden pulled back the curtains, was alive as birds twittered their twilight chorus to the first evening star.

Alison was bending over Mrs Bosquay chafing her hands. "I think she's in a fit of some kind."

Rosanna had dropped into her chair murmuring weakly: "My heart – my heart."

"Get Nurse Duncan," said Eden and I flew upstairs.

When I told her what had happened she rushed down after me complaining, "Lot of silly mumbo-jumbo. Serves them jolly well right. I'm surprised at an intelligent girl like you – " In the drawing room she took Mrs Bosquay's pulse. "She'll live. Best get her home to bed."

"What's the address?" asked Eden.

"It's a fourth-floor tenement," said Alison. "I'll take her."

"You look after Rosanna and Lucy," said Eden.

"Really, this nonsense couldn't have come at a worse time. You'd better be warned, Mr MacAeden has taken a turn apparently for the worse. Dr Poole said I wasn't to leave him and that Hamish would look in later," Nurse Duncan included us all in her angry glance, as if we were somehow responsible for this latest development.

"Can someone please help me upstairs," asked Rosanna crossly, leaning on her stick and conscious that she had only a minor role in this drama. "I feel so ill. My heart, you know. I must go to bed, and I'm leaving this house tomorrow. Nothing would induce me to stay here another day."

"I'll see her to bed," said Alison gently and leading the weeping Rosanna past us, she added, "I'm sorry. I didn't know it would end like this. I did what I thought was best for us all. There's always the danger of picking up elementals, of course. Horrible wasn't it – they tried to strangle poor Drew in Mrs Bosquay's body."

As we helped Mrs Bosquay into Eden's car, she asked in a dazed but rather triumphant fashion, "I got someone, didn't I?" She moved her neck painfully. "Ouch. It's so sore. Was he violent? Who was it?"

"I'll tell you all about it on the way home," said Eden.

Nurse Duncan followed us into the house. "Old fool. Deserves all she gets, tampering with things best left alone. And you two young ones, lending yourselves to this witchcraft," she added severely.

"Never again," said Eden and hugged her.

She smiled at him with a trace of the old flirtatious gleam. "You should both be thinking about more important things. Leave the dead alone."

"We will," said Eden. "Look after Lucy until I get back. Promise?"

"I promise. No bogeyman will get her when I'm around."

Tactfully she went upstairs and Eden said, "Scared?"

I said yes and he smiled. "Go and stay with Nurse Duncan until I get back. I'm not letting you out of my sight until tomorrow morning. I'll be back as quickly as I can." (But it couldn't be less than forty minutes, over to the far side of town and back again, I thought, suddenly afraid.) "Here, take this," he said and dragging down the neck of his sweater he pulled the thunderbird over his head and placed it around my neck. It was still warm. I touched it. "That should keep you safe. A charm against evil."

"Now you *are* scaring me, Eden. It was all trickery, as you said, wasn't it. Even Alison's elementals."

"Elementals?" Eden stared at me, gripped my arms. "I thought you knew . . . You didn't realize? Sweet heaven, Lucy – I don't know what happened this night and I doubt if any of us ever will. I thought I had it all worked out. They were going to pick up Drew and if they didn't, then

Mrs Bosquay was going to rig it. I haven't worked out how they managed Drew so well, but the rest of it . . . They got more than they bargained for with their faked seance to scare you off, Lucy. Those were no elementals."

"Then who was it calling your name?"

Eden held my hands tight. "Lucy, that was Atala. It couldn't have been anyone else. The Atalos language is now so archaic that only about twenty people in the world speak it. And I'm one of them. It was Atala. Unfortunately someone else guessed and scared him off – "

Mrs Bosquay opened the car door, said petulantly, "Are we going soon? I want home. I feel awful."

"Right away," said Eden. "Now remember, do as I say, stay with Nurse Duncan until I get back." And he ran down the steps and into the car.

His fears for me seemed absurd in this houseful of people. I was longing to go over it all with Rosanna and Alison and I was also longing for a cup of coffee. I went into the kitchen, put on the pot, gathered up TeeDee and took her up to the bedroom.

Above the marble fireplace, Janet's portrait smiled at me and the room was very still. If Eden's incredible theory was right and the seance had picked up Atala, perhaps there was reason for the sadness in her eyes tonight, as they followed me with, I fancied, more than their usual intensity. In the gathering gloom, she seemed to take on a strange extra dimension. Almost as if she tried to say something – a warning perhaps. With a shiver I settled TeeDee and went downstairs for the coffee. Returning with my tray I wondered what Alison and Rosanna would make of Atala. It would certainly be a terrible shock, but one that Alison would dine out on for many moons to come. Her positive proof that spiritualism had an honest basis.

I tapped on Rosanna's door. When there was no reply I opened it and said, "Like some coffee?" But Rosanna was already in bed and asleep. She didn't move and the dim light revealed her blonde hair in its sleeping cap sprouting above the covers. Sleep would do her more good than coffee, I thought, closing the door quietly. She must have had a dreadful shock. I wondered if she really intended leaving Lairigbrach, if Alison would miss her or had managed to penetrate that rather baleful personality and discover some warmth beneath it. I'd like to know what made Rosanna tick.

But upstairs I found Alison asleep too. In a chair, still dressed, snoring noisily with her mouth open. "Coffee, Alison." But when I touched her arm, her eyelids flickered and she murmured, "So tired. Lemme sleep."

I felt oddly deflated, and frustrated by wanting to discuss the seance with the main participants, imagining them both arguing into the small hours, enjoying the drama and speculation. But here they both were fast asleep, as if nothing unusual had happened.

I carried my tray along the corridor, tapped on Elliott's door and opened it. Nurse Duncan was sitting in the wingchair, her back turned towards me, the lamp shining on Elliott's still figure in the bed. He looked like a shrivelled effigy in wax, infinitely old, impossible that once could be so old and continue to live.

I tiptoed across and touched her arm, thinking she would want me to wake her when she had dozed off on duty. But she didn't stir. There was a brandy glass on the little table at her side. She smelt strongly of it. How odd, to get drunk on brandy in twenty minutes, she must be a secret drinker. I thought admiringly how well she held her liquor – I would have sworn she was sober when she helped us put Mrs Bosquay into Eden's car.

Rosanna, Alison and now Nurse Duncan. And suddenly for the first time I felt icy cold all over. I was quite alone in Lairigbrach, vulnerable as the heroine of a Victorian melodrama. I could scream as much as I liked, it would have as little effect on the inhabitants of Lairigbrach as on the occupants of Sleeping Beauty's Palace.

No one would heed my cries. *They were all fast asleep*.

I ran into the bedroom, closed the door behind me. But Eden had been mistaken. There was a lock, but no key – yet I seemed to remember a key. Strange, the sash window was half-open – had it been so when I brought TeeDee in only minutes ago?

From the portrait Janet smiled. "The sleeping and the dead are but as pictures," remembering an apt but shiversome quotation from *Macbeth* gave me a nasty jolt. TeeDee sat up panting, showing off her pink tongue in the nearest approach to a human smile, then yawning hugely, she curled up and changed her position for sleep again.

At that moment I heard the sound of running water in the adjoining bathroom, once Janet's dressing room.

"Eden, is that you?" I called.

There were light footsteps and through the door, smiling, drying his face on a pink towel came –

Drew MacAeden.

Chapter 16

"Sit down, Lucy," said Drew, flinging the towel over a chair.

I made a dash for the door but he beat me to it. "Sit down, I said. Don't bother to yell. No one will hear you. Besides, you'll get your chance to scream later, I promise you."

I had to be dreaming. This couldn't happen. Drew was dead.

I blinked as I did so often in nightmares. But the room stayed obstinately the same. The furniture, the curtains, all inanimate objects, they couldn't come running if I called for help. The canopied bed where Eden and I had slept a thousand years ago. . . . Above the marble fireplace, Janet's picture smiled on friend or foe alike.

From her basket, TeeDee raised her head and gave Drew a friendly tailwag of recognition, then bored by humans and their mysterious activities, gave a disinterested yawn and went back to sleep. Not even a dog – this dog – could help me now. Sickened, I forced myself to look at him, knowing that at least this time I wasn't mad, imagining it all.

He stood smiling, running a comb through his hair. "How long has it been, Lucy? Three years? You're even prettier than when I first met you. Perhaps that's what love can do. Have I changed much?" he asked, staring critically at his reflection in the mirror, frowning, always afraid of approaching age, only vulnerable where his vanity was concerned.

He was still the handsomest man I had ever seen, this "angel on the outward side," as Eden had called him. But now the inward side was taking its deadly toll. Changed he undoubtedly had. There was a coarseness, flabbiness of blurred contours, restless eyes that seemed familiar. Then he took out tinted glasses, breathed on them –

I froze. "Rosanna."

"Clever girl," he said mockingly. "That heavy make-up was sheer hell, probably ruined my skin for ever. You'll find all that's left of her, a bolster in the bed and a blonde wig, in her room across the corridor."

"Where is she? The real Rosanna?" For a terrible moment I wondered if he had murdered her, except that Drew always loved himself too much to risk violence that would be punishable. To kill is not for cowards . . .

"Rosanna. She's safely at home with her antiques, of course."

"Then who was killed in the train crash?"

"Tony. Little sod was always borrowing my clothes, as you doubtless remember. His taste was poor, he always envied me and he'd never buy even a tie where he could borrow mine. I was with him when that damned train was derailed at the viaduct. He was nearest the window, killed outright, I remember turning him over, he wouldn't have liked to look like that, his face squashed and mashed about with broken glass.

"That's all I remember about the train. After that, there's a huge blank until I came to myself in a pub forty miles away, with a great bump on my forehead – " he pushed back his hair, "care to feel it? Squeamish, aren't you? I had wandered away suffering from shock, must have got a lift from someone – "

His pathetic glance invited sympathy. I looked away.

Even Drew's subconscious had a built-in survival mechanism. Most of men would instinctively have stayed to help the injured, do what they could for the dying. But not Drew.

"The manager of the pub thought I was stoned. Kept giving me wry looks and arch remarks about, 'How is your hangover this morning, sir?' I had such a splitting headache, I was inclined to believe him. Besides there wasn't a damned thing I could tell him, my name, how I'd got there – until I picked up the newspaper and read about the train crash, two days before."

He laughed. "I nearly scared Rosanna to death when I walked in. Naturally squeamish about blood, she hadn't peered too closely at the body with its face all cut and swollen. She had identified Tony as me and was already collecting my insurance."

"Tony's hair was dark."

Drew smiled. "You're out of date, ducky. He went blonde for a television part last year and decided it was very becoming, so he stayed like that. You know he always wanted to be my twin. He admired me more than anyone else on this earth. I suppose he would have been flattered to death – if you'll excuse the pun – to die as me.

"Well, after I had restored Rosanna, I decided I enjoyed the drama of coming back from the dead. I could have fun with a lot of people who would suffer a lot more than Aunt Rosanna. There would be no complications, I could always plead loss of memory and Tony's family wouldn't make any inquiries. They had disowned him years ago.

"I could always wrap Rosanna round my little finger. She took no persuading, in fact the idea fascinated her, besides it was going to be very embarrassing after her blow-out on my insurance. She was never happier than with a good intrigue on hand, a natural-born weaver of complicated webs and God knows, she had had few of them with a life of paralyzing dullness between here and Australia and her wretched antiques.

"We decided I could lie low as her country cottage was fairly isolated. She wanted me to see a doctor because I was feeling groggy with headaches all the time. But that would have spoilt our plans and besides it was only delayed shock. After two weeks, I thought I'd die of boredom. Then just as I'd decided to declare myself alive again, the victim of a terrible mistake, we heard that Elliott was seriously ill, dying. This set a problem, as you might imagine. Lairigbrach should have come to me, however Rosanna confessed that when she thought I was dead, she'd blabbed about you and the child. Now it appeared from her conversations on the telephone that you had taken Elliott's fancy and he was likely to leave you everything as my next-of-kin.

"Then Rosanna had a brilliant idea. 'If this girl wasn't in the way, Lairigbrach would come to me. We could share it between us. Supposing you scared her off, got her believing she was mad or something. She was always terrified of you – supposing you appeared as Drew's ghost, back to haunt her?"

"I said it was a tricky business and she laughed. 'I'll make it worth your while. You've always enjoyed dressing up in my clothes – I'll bet you five hundred pounds you couldn't fool anyone at Lairigbrach for a week that you are Rosanna. Besides who knows what opportunities might come your way – '"

He sighed. "And it was all working so beautifully, even the rigged seance. Alison is so gullible, she'll believe anything about the supernatural. Then old Bosquay spoilt it all by getting confused and starting on some gibberish with Eden – "

(But it wasn't anything to do with Mrs Bosquay. Eden had told me it was undoubtedly Atala. However the fake seance had been intended to go, they had somehow got more than they bargained for.)

"So – here we are together again, ducky, after many tribulations. Alone at last. Can't say I'm impressed by your sorrowing widow role – you seem positively to have thrived on my demise. Never mind, come and kiss me like a dutiful wife. No?" He laughed. "Thought not. Not to be downhearted. I expect to be around for a very long time and I'm sure I can persuade you to change your mind about your duties as a loving wife."

A loving wife. The past with all its horror flooded back. I was sure he would never let me go. I would never escape from my tormentor.

"Don't look so scared. It would be easy to kill you – "

Could I get past him to the bathroom, lock the door and try to get out of the window. I moved towards the fireplace, but he grabbed me.

"Too easy to kill you," he said firmly. "We'll play some of my games first. You haven't forgotten all the fun we had, have you?" he added softly. Still holding my arm he dragged me to where TeeDee lay and scooped her up in one hand. She gave him an adoring look of frenzied joy as he carried her over to the open window.

"And if you try my patience too much with your silliness," he put out the hand containing TeeDee, "I shall drop her – plop – on to the stones below. A nasty untidy death, much worse than the neat poisoning I planned."

"You – horror."

Ignoring that, he studied me thoughtfully. "And then, of course, you could fall out trying to save her. Or shall I keep you around for a while? What do you think?" As he spoke TeeDee still wagging her tail watched apprehensively the ground far below and gave a frightened whimper.

Eden should be back soon. If only –

"If you think you can keep me talking until Eden comes back – " I gave him a horrified look – "I wouldn't bank on it. Mrs Bosquay was pretty heavily doped too. She'll be fast asleep long before they get to Aberdeen and he's going to have an awful job getting her out of the car and up several flights of stairs. She's a big fat woman, and knowing Eden, he's the conscientious type."

TeeDee was struggling now, crying, terrified. It wasn't such a lovely game after all, her dear loving Rosanna had changed. Only her smell was the same. Drew laughed. "Shall I let her go?"

"No. Please. I'll do anything – "

"That's better." He shook his head sadly. "Only a fool would sacrifice herself for a dog. After all my teaching I thought you would be tougher than that. It's a shame to waste sensitive material like you, ducky. There are so few people in this world who really have hearts that can be broken. Why should I kill you, when I can destroy you inch by inch? It would be much more fun to keep you alive. And I'll never divorce you – keeping you from marrying Eden would be the greatest torment of all."

He threw TeeDee down on her basket and a surprising thing happened. The little dog always so gentle and sweet-natured, took an unexpected revenge on humans who put her out to sea to drown in a shoe-box, who poisoned her lovely chicken and made her ill, who held her above the ground and laughed at her terror. Instead of licking Drew's hand in gratitude for being safely in her basket again, she uttered a low deep growl and sank her teeth savagely into his wrist.

"Little bitch," he screamed in pain. "All right. I know what to do with you – the long drop. Come here." But TeeDee had vanished over the edge of the chair and was far beyond his reach under the bed.

He looked at me, cursing, holding his wrist. "I know what will bring her out. She'll come at me again to save her beloved mistress." Holding my arm with one hand, he lit a cigarette, casual as someone at a cocktail party. "A few nice little burns where they don't show – to start off." And viciously he twisted my arms behind my back and ripped the blouse from my shoulders. The thunderbird on its long chain, swung like a pendulum . . .

Was it only my fear, or had the room grown suddenly still – icy as the drawing-room had been earlier, during the seance? Maybe Drew was aware of it. For a moment he stopped, listened and as his grip on me slackened, I shot away from him towards the door.

But something stopped my hand touching the door handle. It was as if strong arms seized me and turned me bodily round to face Drew's attack.

He stopped inches away, his palms spread out reaching for my throat, face suffused with rage. But his hands never touched me. He groped on air as if a glass barrier lay between us. I saw his eyes looking above my head, widening in terror.

"No. No. Who are you?" he cried.

Then he held a hand in front of him as if to ward off a blow from an unseen assailant and he hurtled across the room to fall with a thud against the marble fireplace. I heard his head crack as he slithered down and lay still.

I knew he was dead instantly, for to that face of a fallen angel turned towards me in death, all evil melted away and innocence returned.

For the space of a single heartbeat I knew I was not alone, there was the shadow of a tall man, and a face I knew and loved. But before I could do more than focus my eyes on him, the door opened. He seemed to glide into the man who rushed in. For an instant there were two of them and then Eden and my strange guardian were one and the same.

Many things happened on the night Drew MacAeden died for the second time. Hamish, whom Eden had met with Mrs Bosquay and who had taken the unfortunate woman

182

into the surgery for treatment from his partner, knelt by Drew's body.

There was no mark or bruise whatever, where his head struck the marble fireplace as he fell. The post-mortem revealed cause of death as delayed fracture of the skull. Without medical attention, from the time of the train accident he had been a doomed man.

The whole truth was never told beyond those nearest to us and only Eden and I knew the events that had taken place between Drew and me in Janet's room. It was reported in the newspapers that Drew's memory had returned and he had come to find his Aunt Rosanna on holiday in Lairigbrach. Unfortunately by the time he reached Scotland she had already left for Dorset again and without any warning, while talking to his shocked "widow", he collapsed and died. It was a sensational story, happening as it did simultaneously with the death that night of Elliott MacAeden, who was probably already dead when I found Nurse Duncan drugged in her chair.

Elliott left Lairigbrach to me, to dispose of as I wished, unaware that Eden and a sympathetic accountant had managed to shield him from the true state of his financial affairs. Bankruptcy was imminent. Ironically, this was in large measure due to the costly litigations over the years as he tried to prove Eden the descendant of Janet MacAeden and Chief Atala, and the rightful heir to Lairigbrach. So to clear the enormous debts, the house was sold to the town as a convalescent home and the balance given to Alison to provide her with a new roof over her head. We felt she deserved it after years of being unpaid housekeeper to Elliott.

Rosanna, after some acid telephone calls and letters in which she vented her spleen on all of us, departed permanently and in high dudgeon to Australia, to live on the proceeds of a fortune made in buying and selling antiques.

Autumn had slid over the Deeside hills and the leaves

183

were already gold as sovereigns fluttering down the tree-lined roads, on the day Eden and I (and TeeDee) left Dyce Airport on the first stage of our journey to Arizona.

Dad, Pearl and the children came to say goodbye. Pearl wistfully envious, believing that we would come back some day as millionaires, refusing to accept that there were also poor Americans. The awful ache of parting from Dad was eased by promised visits. He hugged me repeatedly and finally as he shook hands with Eden, I was content that the two men I loved most regarded each other with respect and affection.

Alison too was there clutching a parcel. "This is your farewell present," she said. "It's the portrait of Atala. I've had it cleaned up and framed. I hope you'll like it, sorry it took so long."

As we waited for the London plane, she took my hand and saw "great happiness in your second marriage, a long life, three children – and some very strange adventures. A fascinating hand, fascinating."

The strange adventures began on the plane as Eden unwrapped the picture and I looked into the face of Atala. A face I knew so well already from the strange dream that was part of my life, the dream that Alison saw written in my hand when I first came to Lairigbrach. It was also Atala I had seen so briefly, the shadowy figure who rescued me from Drew. Atala, who at the fake seance had warned Eden that I was in danger, that he was to take me home to the "red desert" again where I belonged. In the many curious happenings that have made up my life in the years since we left Lairigbrach, one thing has never been explained – why I should be somehow linked with Janet MacAeden and the destiny that led her to Atala a hundred years ago.

As we neared the end of our long journey, Eden took a letter from his briefcase. A long bewildering letter, running into several pages. "Only the last paragraph concerns you at the moment," he said.

The letter proved by lengthy dissertation and genealogical tables proof positive that Eden Atala was undoubtedly the great-grandson of Chief Atala and Janet MacAeden who had been abducted by him.

"Why didn't you tell me before?" I said, for the letter from a New York firm of lawyers was dated two days before Elliott's death.

"I wanted to get away from Lairigbrach. I didn't want arguments – it might have embarrassed Alison. Besides, I was afraid – just a very little – that relationship however remote to the MacAedens, might have frightened you away from me."

The plane swooped low over a land where rocks sprouted from the red earth like the fingers on the submerged hands of a race of forgotten giants. As the engines stopped and we left the plane, we could see a small crowd had gathered to wait quietly, their faces unsmiling.

Waiting for Eden. The Navajos and Atalos from the reservation that would be our home. The people who were his people, who believed he had come to fulfil a prophecy, ancient as their own heritage.

One day (said the prophecy) the Sacred One, the Sun-God of the Atalos would descend from the sky in a great winged chariot. From his own hands he would spread life back in a desert land. Where he walked, trees and plants would grow where none had grown before. His people would forget the taste of bitterness and become great again, as the Atalos had been in the days before their other world sank beneath the great ocean . . .

I looked at Eden. The setting sun threw shadows of cheekbone and jaw on to a face suddenly alien. Strip off that dark suit, the white shirt, the psychedelic tie and he would be "The Warrior" of Alison's painting. Put on a gold headdress and a few arm ornaments and he was the Sacred One, remote, inhuman . . .

I knew fear then. Could this Barbaric Stranger be

my husband, the lover whom I held in my arms? And then I remembered the happiness of these months past, happiness I had never expected to know in this life. He reached out, took my hand, nervously twisting the thick gold wedding ring and I thought of a love that was kind and gentle too, a love that knew, besides the joy of fulfilment, laughter and abiding tenderness.

He looked down at me, straightened his shoulders and smiled.

"Scared?"

"A little."

"Me, too," said the Sun-God of the Atalos. "There's a lot to do, but somehow we'll suceed – together. I need you and I love you."

And so Chief Eden Atala, B.Sc (Agriculture) Ph.D., Laird of Lairigbrach, went home again.